"I Want Kids. You Want Kids. We're Both Prepared To Do Some Unorthodox Things To Get Them."

Quentin took a few steps away, then turned back to face Liz. "I haven't been looking to become a father. But I'm a businessman and I'd be a fool to pass down a good deal."

A good deal. That's what she'd been reduced to. "What sort of deal?"

"We're two adults who are attracted to each other. You want a baby." He blew out a breath. "And I'll eventually want kids, too."

"Eventually?"

"Yeah. I hadn't been planning on getting married. At least, not the traditional love-and-happily-ever-after variety."

"You don't have to be married to have kids."

"In my book you do."

"What are you saying, Quentin?"

"I'm saying, let's give it a shot. Four dates. At the end of it, we decide whether we like each other enough to get married and have a kid together. Right away."

Dear Reader,

When it comes to passion, Silhouette Desire has exactly what you need. This month's offerings include Cindy Gerard's *The Librarian's Passionate Knight,* the next installment of DYNASTIES: THE BARONES. A naive librarian gets swept off her feet by a dashing Barone sibling—who could ask for anything more? But more we do have, with another story about attractive and wealthy men, from Anne Marie Winston. *Billionaire Bachelors: Gray* is a deeply compelling story about a man who gets a second chance at life—and maybe the love of a lifetime.

Sheri WhiteFeather is back this month with the final story in our LONE STAR COUNTRY CLUB trilogy. *The Heart of a Stranger* will leave you breathless when a man with a sordid past gets a chance for ultimate redemption. Launching a new series this month is Kathie DeNosky with *Lonetree Ranchers: Brant.* When a handsome rancher helps a damsel in distress, all his defenses come crashing down and the fun begins.

Silhouette Desire is pleased to welcome two brand-new authors. Nalini Singh's *Desert Warrior* is an intense, emotional read with an alpha hero to die for. And Anna DePalo's *Having the Tycoon's Baby*, part of our ongoing series THE BABY BANK, is a sexy romp about one woman's need for a child and the sexy man who grants her wish—but at a surprising price.

There's plenty of passion rising up here in Silhouette Desire this month. So dive right in and enjoy.

Melissa Jeglinski

Melissa Jeglinski
Senior Editor
Silhouette Desire

Please address questions and book requests to:
Silhouette Reader Service
U.S.: 3010 Walden Ave., P.O. Box 1325, Buffalo, NY 14269
Canadian: P.O. Box 609, Fort Erie, Ont. L2A 5X3

Having the Tycoon's Baby

ANNA DePALO

Silhouette® Desire

Published by Silhouette Books

America's Publisher of Contemporary Romance

SILHOUETTE BOOKS

ISBN 0-373-76530-4

HAVING THE TYCOON'S BABY

This edition published by arrangement with Harlequin Books S.A.

Visit Silhouette at www.eHarlequin.com

Printed in U.S.A.

ANNA DePALO

A lifelong book lover, Anna discovered that she was a writer at heart when she realized that not everyone travels around with a full cast of characters in her head. She has lived in Italy and England, learned to speak French, graduated from Harvard, earned graduate degrees in political science and law, forgotten how to speak French and married her own dashing hero.

When not writing, Anna is an intellectual-property lawyer in New York City. She loves traveling, reading, writing, old movies, chocolate and Italian (which she hasn't forgotten how to speak, thanks to her extended Italian family). She's thrilled to be writing for Silhouette. Readers can visit her at www.annadepalo.com.

To my family and friends,
particularly my parents, Enza and Frank,
and my husband, Colby,
for encouraging me to
pursue every dream.

One

"**I**'m calling a sperm bank and getting artificially inseminated."

Liz Donovan's pronouncement was met with a mixture of surprise and disbelief. Allison Whittaker, her best friend of more than ten years, was the person exhibiting the emotions in question.

They were sitting in the book-lined study of Allison's parents' house, an impressive redbrick colonial on the outskirts of the town of Carlyle, just northeast of Boston. Each year the Whittaker family hosted a Memorial Day Weekend barbecue and this year was no exception, even though Allison's parents, Ava and James, were traveling in Europe.

"But, Lizzie, the baby will never know its father. Doesn't that bother you?"

"Yes, but a sperm bank seems like my best choice

right now. Besides, I'll be able to pick eye color, height, everything I want.''

Allison was the person who had accompanied her to the hospital a few weeks ago when she'd had the outpatient laparoscopic surgery that had confirmed her gynecologist's diagnosis—and Liz's worst fear: endometriosis.

Fortunately, hers was a mild case, discovered early, and the short surgery had removed most of the offending implants around her uterus. But, there was no telling what the future would hold. Which meant, of course, that she'd be spinning the gaming wheel each year she waited to have a child—if it wasn't too late already.

Allison frowned. "Wouldn't you rather use someone you know?'' she argued. "Knowing who the father is has got to be a big advantage.''

Liz sighed. A part of her still couldn't believe that her time for having a baby might be running out. She wouldn't even turn thirty for another six months!

Having a family of her own had always been important to her: her mother had died when she was eight and she'd been an only child. Frankly, if she hadn't had such a burning desire to prove to herself and her overprotective father that she could and would succeed in the business world, she might have paid less attention to her career and more to the state of her basically nonexistent social life.

In fact, work was partly why she was at the Whittaker mansion today, despite the upheaval of the last couple of weeks. She was hoping to have a chance to discuss a big account for her interior design business,

Precious Bundles, which specialized in children's rooms and play areas.

Allison had suggested that she do the design for the new day care planned for Whittaker Enterprises' headquarters. If she got the contract, it would be Precious Bundles' biggest account to date and would bring her one step closer—one big step closer, she corrected herself—to getting her business on a sound financial footing.

With any luck, Allison's brother Quentin, the CEO of Whittaker Enterprises, would show up soon and she'd have a chance to seal the deal.

Liz determinedly pushed away the twinge of nervousness that usually accompanied any thoughts of Quentin and reached for the glass of lemonade that she'd set down on the coffee table. "Of course there are advantages to knowing the father, but who would I use? I'm not seeing anyone, and I don't have any close male friends."

Allison seemed pensive for a moment, then offered, "Well, I've got three brothers."

Liz's hand stilled, half to the glass, and she looked at Allison with a mixture of horror and amusement. "You're giving me nightmare visions of some teenaged schemes you got me involved in."

"You loved every minute of them!" Allison pretended to look offended.

Liz sat back against the cushions of the couch, the glass forgotten, and heaved another sigh. Allison could be tenacious. It was a trait that served her well as a hotshot Assistant District Attorney in Boston, but it also made her tough to argue with. "Even you have to admit that volunteering one of your brothers for sperm donor duty is a little on the wild side."

"Why?" Allison got up and started pacing. "It makes perfect sense. My mother has been pushing for a grandchild, but none of my brothers shows any signs of delivering the goods, so to speak. And I'm not about to marry any boring 'so-and-so the Third' to make her happy!" Allison stopped and gave her a winning smile. "Besides, I know you'll make a wonderful mother. The best, in fact."

"The best what?" asked a deep voice from the doorway.

Liz tensed and gave Allison a warning look.

Even after eleven years, Quentin Whittaker, the oldest of Allison's three older brothers, hadn't lost the power to make her nervous and skittish. Tall, at least six-two by Liz's estimate, with raven-black hair cut conservatively short, he had strong and even features marred only by a small scar at the corner of his right brow—the result of a hockey accident in college.

His eyes connected with hers across the study. "Hello, Elizabeth."

He never called her Liz, like most people did, or Lizzie, which was what family and close friends sometimes used.

It occurred to her that they'd first met in this room, in this house: she'd been eighteen and on the verge of graduating from high school and he'd been a twenty-five-year-old on the verge of graduating from Harvard Business School.

One look into his bottomless light-gray eyes and she'd been flying through the heavens, borne on the wings of teenaged lust and longing. Quentin, on the other hand, had seemed immune, then and in later meetings, treating her with polite reserve.

He moved into the room, heading for the huge mahogany desk sitting in front of picture windows at the side of the room. "The best what?" he repeated, addressing his question to Allison.

"Quent, Liz needs to have a baby. Fast."

"Allison!" Liz gaped at her friend. She'd forgotten how Ally could be like a dog with a bone when it came to one of her "ideas."

Quentin halted and frowned. *"What?"*

"The doctor told her today that she has endometriosis. The longer she waits to have a baby, the more likely it is that she'll never have one."

Quentin eyes pinned Liz to her seat. "Is that true?"

"Yes," she heard herself say in a strangled voice.

Allison ignored the quelling look that Liz threw her way. "She needs a sperm donor."

Quentin's eyes narrowed. "My hunch is that the reason you're telling me this is you're looking for a sperm donor?"

Allison rushed on, seemingly oblivious to Quentin's ominous tone. "Quentin, you've been getting a lot of pressure from Mom and Dad to settle down and produce a grandchild. And, you've said yourself you have no intention of getting close to the altar again. The way I see it, this is a solution to both your problems."

"Allison, please!" Liz could feel her face turning redder. She was mortified that her friend would suggest that Quentin, of all men, father her baby. And from the looks of it, Quentin looked equally horrified at the prospect.

"You don't know what you're asking," Quentin said to his sister. The expression on his face spoke volumes, including, clearly, that he thought that his sister had lost her mind.

Liz let out the breath she'd been holding. She'd been insane to think for an instant that Quentin would jump at the chance to father her baby.

"I don't know what I'm asking?" Allison asked, surveying her brother's charcoal-gray suit and blue tie with clear disapproval. "It's Saturday, Quent—Memorial Day Weekend—and where have you been? Working as usual, it seems. And if I know you, you came in to the study looking to do more work. I'd say I know exactly what I'm saying."

Liz stifled her rising panic. "Quentin, I want you to know I didn't ask Allison to bring this up." She shook her head when Allison opened her mouth. "In fact, I told Allison that I'd be making an appointment with a sperm bank."

Quentin swung to face her. "Have you both gone crazy?" He stuffed his hands in his front pants pockets. "I thought Allison's idea was a little off the wall, but—" he growled "—now I realize she's the more rational of the two of you."

Liz felt heat rise into her face. "A sperm bank is a perfectly reasonable idea. Many women choose it."

"You're not many women," he retorted.

Since when had he become an expert on what type of woman she was or wasn't? As far as she could tell, he'd acted for years as if he didn't know she was a woman!

She rose from her seat. She'd always found Quentin a bit intimidating, but her temper was getting the best of her. "I'll be the judge of that. After all, it's my problem!"

"What have you got to say to that, huh, Quent?" Allison piped in.

Quentin threw his sister a warning look before zeroing in on Liz again. "Why don't you just get married? What's wrong with that? Just find yourself a nice guy, and go make babies."

Liz sighed with exasperation. "Just like that, hmm?" She snapped her fingers. "And where do you suggest I find Mr. Nice?"

"Pick a guy," he bit out. "We're all easy prey."

"Oh, really? Well, perhaps that's the way you see it, but the view from over here is a lot different." She started counting on her fingers. "Let's see. It'll take a few months to meet someone suitable. Then a couple of weeks for dating."

She took a breath. "Third or fourth date, I let him have his wicked way with me."

A muscle started to tick in Quentin's jaw.

"That's about right, wouldn't you say, Quentin? After all, you guys are always complaining about how long the chase is."

"Elizabeth—" he said warningly.

She knew she was baiting him in a way she'd never dared do. It was reckless, but she didn't care. Maybe it was her medical diagnosis, but something had been unleashed within her. "Okay, now we're at about one month into the relationship. No time to waste, so I propose to him."

She was on the verge of losing control, but all the despair she'd tried to keep carefully hidden was welling to the surface. "Let's say I'm lucky and the first man I propose to actually likes me enough to marry me. Well, we'll need a few weeks to plan a quickie ceremony in front of a judge."

"Elizabeth—"

She held up her hand to stop him. "At this point, four or five months at least have gone by. But he's so taken with me, he agrees to have a baby right away! Well, that's going to take a few months of trying."

She paused for breath. She was starting to sound hysterical. "So, I'd say, six to seven months if everything goes *perfectly*."

Quentin's fists bunched and he looked tight-lipped and grim. She knew she'd pushed him, but she was beyond caring.

"Listen, Elizabeth, I don't know what Allison told you, but I'm not in the market for fatherhood. I'm sure my mother would love to become a grandmother, but she has three others who can help her there."

Allison coughed, and they both turned to glare at her. "Oh, come on, Quentin. You know Mom and Dad have been pressuring you for ages. And it's not just because they want a grandkid. They're worried about you. Ever since—"

Quentin cut her off. "My private life is healthy enough, thanks for asking."

Healthy? Well, that was one way to put it. Quentin's private life had been prime grist for the Boston papers for years. If past record was anything to judge by, he preferred statuesque and glamorous career women with sleek pageboy do's, and model-perfect size-eight figures.

She, on the other hand, was so far from being his "type" that it was laughable. Her unruly chestnut hair fell below her shoulders, the thick, curling locks tending to frizziness. And her figure...well, she'd made repeated vows to shed those stubborn five pounds, but they seemed to have found a permanent home on her hips.

"Look, this isn't just a matter of a sperm donation. I'd want to be a father, not just some stud, to my kid," Quentin continued.

"Exactly." Liz shot a quelling look at Allison. "That's why a sperm bank is such a good idea."

"No!" Quentin and Allison shot out.

"Look, there's got to be another solution," Quentin said in exasperation.

"Another solution for what?" Matthew Whittaker, the middle Whittaker brother, asked as he sauntered into the room from the doorway leading to the front hall.

His question was greeted with stony silence.

Matthew's gaze swung from a frowning Quentin to an excited Allison, before coming to rest on Liz. He held up his hands. "Hey, don't everybody answer at once!"

"Lizzie's got a problem," Allison finally volunteered.

Matthew cocked a brow. "Oh, really? What sort of problem?"

"Yeah, what sort of problem?" Noah Whittaker, the third Whittaker brother, appeared in the doorway behind Matthew. He winked at Liz. "Hey, beautiful."

"Lizzie needs to get pregnant fast or she may never have a baby."

"Allison," Liz said sternly.

"Damn." Matthew shot Liz a sympathetic look. "What're the options?"

Allison gave her brother a level look. "Funny you should ask—"

"Well, if everyone in this family must know," Liz jumped in before Allison had a chance to speak, "I was asking for advice about a reputable sperm bank."

"Gonna go it alone, are you?"

Liz sighed in relief. Finally, an ally. "Yes."

"Congratulations."

"You'll make a great mama," Noah added.

Liz saw Allison throw her brothers a reproachful look.

Matthew looked perplexed. "What?"

"You just picked showcase number wrong," Allison quipped.

"At least we agree on that," Quentin said in a sardonic tone.

"Matt," Allison continued, "wouldn't it be great if Liz could use someone she knew instead? Say a family friend?"

Liz saw Matthew hold his sister's gaze for an instant, then lounge back against the door frame and fold his arms as if he were contemplating Allison's question. "Well, I'd say that would be a good idea."

"Right," Quentin said tightly. "I have an even better one. How about using a husband?"

"Liz doesn't have one, Quent," Noah pointed out with his typical lazy humor.

"Well, then she can damn well get one pronto."

"Tsk. Tsk." Matthew shook his head. "Don't you know women have choices these days, Neanderthal man?"

Liz could see that didn't go over well with Quentin. He gave Matthew a hard stare. "If you've got something to say, Matt," he said coolly, "I suggest you just spit it out."

Matthew regarded all the occupants of the room before saying, "Well, I'd say it's obvious. Lizzie needs a male friend she can trust, and I'm hands-down the best guy she knows." He winked encouragingly at Liz. "Honey, as long as I don't have to fill the whole turkey baster, I'm your man."

Quentin recovered with amazing speed. It was something he was known for. He'd been a star hockey player at prep school, and then at Harvard, due in no small measure to his quick reflexes. They also made him a formidable adversary in the boardroom. Always look prepared. Never be seen with your guard down.

He turned on his brother. "Are you nuts?"

"Not at all. Are you?" Matt returned mildly.

Noah swallowed a chuckle.

"You can't father Elizabeth's baby."

"Last time I checked all the parts were in working order."

Quentin's fists tightened. He couldn't remember the

last time he'd wanted to rearrange Matt's face. "You know what I mean, dammit."

"I don't know why you're annoyed, Quent," Allison piped up from the sofa. "After all, you're not interested."

Elizabeth saved him from a scathing reply. "I appreciate that you're all trying to—" she hesitated as her gaze met his "—help." She turned to Matt. "Thanks for the offer. But I've always thought of you as a brother. Let's not complicate the great friendship we have, okay?"

Matt smiled, admiration lighting his eyes. "Okay, but if you ever reconsider—"

"Thanks," Elizabeth said softly, then cleared her throat.

Quentin frowned. Why didn't she ever give him those soft looks? They'd known each other—what?— more than ten years.

Maybe it was him. He'd been annoyed as all hell the first time he'd caught himself having a physical reaction to her. She'd been just barely eighteen at the time and still a kid in his book.

Of course, that was ages ago. Before Vanessa had taught him no woman could be trusted.

His lips twisted at the thought of his ex-fiancée. At least she'd taught him a valuable lesson. To single women, he was just a big ol' pot of gold with a wedding band sitting on top of it.

Unfortunately, his brother hadn't wised up yet. Poor guy probably thought it was his charm that had all those women in hot pursuit.

"Matt, Elizabeth won't be changing her mind." He ignored Allison's frown. "She'll find a solution."

"I'm sure I will," said Elizabeth a bit stiffly. "Excuse me, will you?" she asked of no one in particular as she left the room.

"How could you!"

His gaze shifted from the doorway to his irate sister. "How could I what?"

"You could have shown a little sympathy."

He pushed aside the twinge of guilt. "I did." Then added, "But I'd say asking for a sperm donation is more than just a little sympathy." He then turned to Matt, who was still looking at him obliquely. "We need to discuss Project Topaz as soon as this shindig is over."

Matt gave a sardonic salute. "Yes, sir."

"Wisea—"

"Thanks," Matt interrupted, a laughing glimmer in his eye, then jerked his thumb at their brother, "but you have me confused with Noah."

Noah raised his hands and took a step back. "Keep me out of this one."

Quentin arched a brow—in his opinion, Matt could give Noah a run for the money in the smart aleck department. Wisely, though, he decided not to offer up his opinion. Instead, he strode from the room before Allison could start the argument she was obviously itching to have with him.

By tacit agreement, he and Elizabeth avoided each other for the rest of the afternoon. She bore up well under the stress, he noted. She oohed and aahed over Mrs. Cassidy's knitting. She pushed their neighbor's five-year-old daughter Millicent on the tree swing, and relieved Noah in a game of catch with Millicent's twin brother Tommy. She blushed as praise was heaped on her apple pies.

She ignored him.

He didn't know why the idea of Elizabeth using a sperm bank should bother him so much, he thought while he watched her chat with Noah. Maybe it was because the damn things made him—and all men, for that matter—seem so unnecessary.

But it wasn't as if he had a personal stake in the matter—other than the fact that she'd been a friend of the family for years, and everyone seemed to adore her.

The sane thing for him to do was to avoid getting involved. The best way to do that, of course, was to avoid her. Unfortunately, he'd already committed to working with her on the planned site for the day care.

Two

Quentin always thought his office was immense, but it was starting to feel about as large as a broom closet. Elizabeth had arrived to discuss the details of the day-care construction.

His gaze swept over her again. A conservative blue suit clung to generous curves. Black pumps showed off a shapely set of legs, which, at the moment, were crossed at the ankle and tucked to the side of her as she sat, pad in hand and jotting notes.

He suspected wryly that she'd be disappointed to discover the overall effect was of a poorly disguised siren.

He was glad she'd shown up and appeared ready to put Saturday behind them. In fact, they seemed to be back to their old polite but distant relationship.

And that's just the way he wanted it, he told himself.

"May I tour the site for the day care now?" she asked politely.

"Of course." He rose from his seat and could have sworn she looked alarmed.

"Are you going to show me around?"

He arched a brow. "Yes, is that a problem?"

"No, no," she said quickly, depositing her writing pad and pen in her leather purse. "It's just I know you're busy, and I'm sure there's someone else you could ask."

"Well, the day care is an important project, isn't it?"

She darted him a quick look, but before he could interpret it, she'd started out of his office.

A mixture of curiosity and the need to fill the silence made him ask, "How long have you been on your own? You used to be with one of those big design firms in Boston."

"It's been two or three years."

"Things didn't go well in Boston?"

He silently berated himself for the obvious negative assumption behind that question, but she didn't seem to take offense. "No, not that," she replied. "I just always knew I wanted to run my own business."

Now that, he could identify with. He'd spent the past several years expanding Whittaker Enterprises and multiplying his net worth. He guessed he shouldn't be surprised that, while he'd been occupied with his career and hadn't seen much of Elizabeth, she'd been moving forward with her life as well.

The elevator opened on the ground floor and he led the way to the northeastern-most section of the building.

The room was large, sunlight streaming through the floor-length windows that faced the lawn at the back of the building.

"This is wonderful!" Elizabeth exclaimed, her voice proclaiming that she was pleasantly surprised.

Quentin supposed that comment reflected badly on the level of interest he'd shown in the construction of the day-care center, but aloud he just said, "I'm glad you approve." He leaned against the door frame, crossed his arms and watched her as she moved gracefully across the room.

Two paint-stained ladders sat on a tarpaulin at one end of the room. The painters he'd hired had been covering and smoothing over holes in the walls. The room had housed dozens of cubicles, and computer wire and cable had run everywhere.

She glanced back over her shoulder at him, her face alight with possibilities. "My initial idea is to create a door where one of the floor-length windows is now and create a small outdoor play area. Enclosed by a fence, of course." She paused, then added, "Do you think that'll work?"

"I don't think it'll be a problem to give up a little lawn."

"And it gives the kids a direct exit in case of fire. So that will be another advantage."

"Good."

"We'll need to set up cubbyholes against one wall."

"Cubbyholes?"

"Yes," she said patiently, "so parents can store things for their kids. You know, like diapers, bibs."

"Right." She could have told him they needed space suits and a couple of rocket ships, and he'd have taken her word for it.

He wracked his brain. Preschool was a vague and hazy memory. Had they had—what did she call them—cubbyholes?

"—kitchen?" Elizabeth finished.

"What?" He pushed away from the door frame.

"I said," she repeated, "you know we'll have to put in a small kitchen or pantry. And bathrooms."

He nodded. "I guess we can't have little Johnny standing in line behind some business executive to use the facilities."

A smile touched her lips. "Exactly. You know more than you think you do."

He brought his finger to his lips. "Shh. Don't let the word get out."

She laughed then, her eyes merry, the light glinting off her hair as she turned back to him.

She was gorgeous. Time—when he hadn't been paying attention—had been good to her. How hadn't he noticed? And *why* hadn't he?

It seemed impossible that Elizabeth was facing infertility. She exuded the Earth Mother. Her lush curves bordered on voluptuous.

The white blouse she wore under her open suit jacket clearly defined her large breasts and just hinted at the lacy bra that supported them. While her straight blue skirt ended, appropriately enough, just above her knees, it also allowed a display of shapely legs, showcased in clear hose and high-heeled black pumps.

His only disagreement was with her hairstyle: she had hidden her thick, long auburn hair in a businesslike knot. He wondered what she would say if he asked her to take it down, then felt his blood heat at the thought.

She started walking back to where he was standing. "Is that all?" he asked, keeping his voice even, although his body felt tight and all too aware of her.

"Oh, yes-s!"

Her exclamation ended in a gasp as she stumbled. Instinctively, he reached out to break her fall, catching her against him. He almost groaned aloud as her soft breasts collided with his chest.

Her face jerked up to his, her eyes wide, her face flushing with embarrassment. "I think my heel caught on something!"

He forced himself to look past her to the floor. "Definitely a crack. Must have been caused by the repair work. Looks like the floor will need a touchup job." His eyes came back to hers.

She gave a weak laugh. "I'll have to be more careful. Otherwise *I'll* need a touch-up job."

She must have read something in his gaze, because suddenly all attempts at amusement faded and a stiffness came back to her shoulders. Her eyes widened— a fascinating shade of green flecked with bits of gold, one slightly more than the other—and her lips parted, drawing his gaze down to them.

They looked full, wet and infinitely kissable. Instinctively, he bent his head.

A look of alarm came into her eyes and she quickly braced her hands on his chest. "I–I'll have some design plans in the next week or so," she said a bit breathlessly.

Abruptly, his head cleared and he dropped his arms so she could take a step back. "Right."

She straightened her handbag on her shoulder. "I—I'll call as soon as I have some plans done."

She couldn't escape fast enough after that.

Quentin swore silently as he watched her go.

Damn, damn. What had gotten into him? He'd been about to kiss her in the middle of his office building, in the middle of the day! Was he nuts? He hadn't seen her in a long while before the barbecue at his parents' place, but he'd known her for ages.

Of course, this was the first time she'd literally fallen into his arms! Still, he wasn't the seize-the-opportunity type. And Elizabeth had enough problems without having him add a lecherous employer to the mix.

He was still trying to come up with a good rationalization for what had almost happened when he sat down to his lunch meeting with Noah later that day.

"How did it go this morning?" Noah asked, reaching for the breadbasket lying on the conference room table.

"Everything's under control," he said nonchalantly without looking up from a memo the research and development department had sent him. "But I don't have time for it, so count on the day care being your project from now on."

"A real babe, isn't she?"

He didn't even pretend to not understand his brother's meaning. He gave Noah a hard look. "Elizabeth is soon going to be under contract. She's a business associate. And a friend of the family."

"Oh, come on, Quentin. You can't tell me you didn't notice those big green eyes and that sexy wa—"

"And I told you to keep your hands—and everything else for that matter—off of her." Not that he'd set a sterling example that morning, he reminded himself ruefully.

"Okay, you're the boss," Noah responded with an easygoing grin.

"Yeah, try to remember that for more than fifteen seconds."

After his encounter with Elizabeth that morning he'd decided the safest course was to get someone else to handle the day-care center. Not hiring Elizabeth wasn't an option—Allison would give him hell.

The obvious solution was to make sure Noah got this whole project finished ASAP. Much as his brother was making him regret that decision at the moment.

"You know," Noah was saying, "I was just kidding. Allison explained Liz's medical condition to me. Rotten luck."

Quentin knew his brother well enough not to dance around what was obviously on Noah's mind. "Of course Allison's harebrained solution would be creating a new subsidiary, Whittaker Spermbanks R Us."

Noah grinned. "Yeah." He poured himself some

water from the pitcher on the conference table. "Started off with the wrong brother though."

"Not you, too."

Noah shrugged. "You've walked the straight and narrow too long. Your idea of radical is wearing a tie with broad stripes."

"This from the guy who pestered me for weeks for an introduction to Samantha the Sweater Girl?" Quentin asked, pretending to look incredulous.

"That was high school, maybe college. You missed the turn to the uber-cool thirties a long time ago and just kept on going."

Quentin shook his head. "Great, I'm square, or whatever they're calling uncool these days."

"Look, all I'm saying is that donating sperm is not such an off-the-wall idea. We've known Liz for a long time. Helping her out—"

"For cripes' sake, you talk about it like it's offering to fix her leaky faucet!"

"Okay, it's different. And I'm not saying you should do it."

"Matt—"

Noah shook his head. "He hasn't said anything. Ally told me what he said at the barbecue, but he hasn't mentioned it since then that I know of."

Quentin felt himself releasing the tension he hadn't even known he had.

Noah gave him a quizzical look. "You should have gone for her when she was younger and visiting Allison all the time. I could have sworn she had a crush on you."

Ignoring Quentin's dark look, Noah continued irrepressibly, "God knows why though. There were far better specimens of male prowess hanging around the house. Women, go figure!"

"She was a kid!"

Noah eyed him speculatively. "Well, she's not anymore."

"Well, she's a business associate now."

"Yeah, but that won't last forever. And you do seem to be acting uncharacteristically passionate on the topic of Lizzie and insemination, Quent."

"You're barking up the wrong tree. I just don't want her to do something she'll regret. Call me old-fashioned, but I believe in making babies the traditional way."

If Noah was skeptical about that, he kept his thoughts to himself. "Allison's idea isn't so crazy, Quent. Mom has been after you for little Whittakers."

Quentin rolled his eyes. "Don't go there."

"All right, bro," Noah wiggled his eyebrows, "but you wouldn't have to donate sperm if you can convince Liz to do it the old-fashioned way."

Quentin nearly lost control of the cup of coffee he'd picked up. He set it down on its saucer with a clatter. "Oh, great, seduce my kid sister's best friend. I see that working out."

"All I'm saying is, why don't you take a closer look. This might be a long-term investment that's worth making."

Try as she might to concentrate on work, Liz found her mind replaying the events in Quentin's office. Quentin had been about to kiss her. That much was clear. And she, like a ninny, had reacted like a deer caught in headlights: wide-eyed and then bolting as fast as she could.

She sighed. It figured that, after all these years, when finally presented with the opportunity she used to fantasize about, she'd completely blow it. She just wasn't the cool and collected sophisticated type.

What remained a mystery was just why Quentin had almost kissed her. Was he curious about whether he'd be able to feel any attraction for her at all?

What would have happened if he had kissed her? She shivered, the thought sending prickles of aware-ness through her.

Then she stopped abruptly. What was she doing? She'd gotten over her infatuation with Quentin years ago, she told herself firmly. And nothing good could come of unlocking that door again, particularly now that she was working for him.

She should just be glad Quentin had decided to let her have the day-care project despite her totally un-professional behavior at the barbecue on Saturday. The Whittaker account was really going to help her cash flow situation.

Her eyes strayed for the umpteenth time to the bro-chures at the corner of her wide Victorian desk, parked near the bay windows at the front of the first story of her house. The brochures had started to arrive from various fertility clinics in Boston.

Her initial panic and shock at the doctor's news had faded, but her bravado was also deserting her. How was she ever going to manage all by herself? A fledg-ling business, a new baby and a mortgage on a rambling old Victorian house that still needed lots of work.

Even the artificial insemination was going to cost money. She'd received a small inheritance from her Aunt Kathleen that she'd intended to squirrel away as a nest egg. As painful as the thought was, however, she'd probably need to use that money for the sperm bank.

Her thoughts were interrupted by the ringing phone. "Hello?"

"Hey beautiful, your prince has come."

Her lips quirked. "Well hello, prince. How are you?"

"Trying to keep five balls in the air as one of Quentin's loyal deputies." Noah gave a dramatic groan. "Got to reschedule our meeting for Monday. Looks like I'm going to have to be out of town again. If you're available, how about a working dinner tomorrow night instead?"

She couldn't resist teasing, "That would be Friday night. I'd have thought you'd have plans."

"I do, sweetness, I do," Noah drawled in a parody of seductiveness. "And that's to take a beautiful green-eyed brunette to the best French restaurant in Boston."

Since she'd always had an easy relationship with Noah, she wondered if one of his motives wasn't to cheer her up. Their meeting wasn't urgent and could wait until he returned to town. Aloud she said, "Who told you I love French food?"

"I have my sources. I'll pick you up at nine."

"Wonderful."

The next night Noah had her smiling the minute she opened her door, as he staggered back a step, clutching his chest. "Be still my heart. My dreams have been answered."

"Oh, you clown." She was wearing a short-sleeved blue cocktail dress, one she'd had at the back of her closet. Still, it was nice to be appreciated.

The maitre d' at Beauchamp greeted Noah like an old friend. Obviously, the upscale restaurant was a favorite. They were seated at a candlelit table near windows affording a view of the Charles River.

"I'm on strict orders to discuss costs and contracts tonight, but," Noah said, winking, "let's leave the boring stuff for after dinner."

"That's the way of it, is it?" Liz returned playfully. "Wine-and-dine me, and soften me up."

"You wound me."

"Au contraire. I just don't want you to waste your time."

Noah grinned. "Dinner with a lovely woman is never a waste of time."

She laughed despite herself until she looked into Quentin's eyes across the restaurant and froze. Allison had entered at his side.

Noah turned to follow her gaze and rose as his brother and sister approached, Allison leading the way, followed by the maitre d' and a forbidding-looking Quentin.

"What a pleasant surprise!" Allison exclaimed. Turning to Quentin, she prompted, "Isn't it?"

"Quite," he said dryly.

"Do you mind if we join you?"

"Not at all," Liz murmured. Quentin looked impressive and forbidding in a dark gray suit. She experienced the little flutter in her stomach and quivery tension that she'd always felt whenever he was near.

"Actually, I do mind," Noah spoke up and Liz threw him a startled look. "You're going to cramp my style. So beat it, kid."

Allison laughed and swatted her brother.

Liz felt her face heat. She stole a look at Quentin, who looked even more grim if that were possible. She cringed at the thought of how this must appear, and what he was thinking.

They were moved to a table for four by the deft and efficient maitre d'. Quentin sat himself across from Elizabeth, who seemed to be reading the menu with the fascination one would accord to the climactic scene of a potboiler bestseller. Uncomfortable, was she?

His eyes traveled to her lips, which were looking *only* slightly pouty this evening, he decided. The dress she was wearing revealed a creamy expanse which sloped gently down before leveling off at two perfect globes that strained against the confining fabric of her bodice.

His hands itched to release them from their confinement and weigh them in his palms, stroking his thumbs over nipples that would harden and darken at his touch....

Realizing the direction his mind was heading, he mentally braked.

Was he crazy?

He had no business speculating about her breasts—
even if his overactive imagination insisted on supply-
ing details to his fevered mind.

The woman had to be stopped.

He had to hand it to her though, she was a fast
worker. Last week she was propositioning him, this
week she was already moving on to fairer game.
Maybe she preferred Noah—they'd always had a flir-
tatious banter. Maybe that's really why she'd found it
so easy to say no to Matt. She already knew who her
target was, and the sperm bank idea was a smoke-
screen.

Or maybe he'd convinced her with his arguments
about finding a husband. The problem was he hadn't
meant his brother.

He looked at Noah. His brother was susceptible to
beautiful women. He'd be a sucker for one in need.
He might not mind obliging....

"Don't you think so, Quentin?"

"What?"

Allison's eyes met his, amusement in their depths,
as if she had been reading his mind. "I was saying
we should order some of the vintage Chardonnay.
That's a weakness you share with Liz." She turned
to Liz. "Any suggestions?"

"I'm sure Quentin will make an excellent choice."
Liz glanced at Quentin then and he gave the barest
dip of his head in acknowledgment of what she'd said.

She wondered if Noah and Allison were as aware
of the tension in the air as she was. As she passed the
butter, her fingers accidentally brushed Quentin's, and
she snatched her hand back, as if singed, nearly up-

setting the small plate in the process. Quentin merely raised a brow questioningly.

During dinner, Noah asked her a few softball questions about the details of the day care. Once or twice her eyes connected with Quentin's, but he declined to add anything.

"How is Patrick liking the fly-fishing down in Florida?" Allison asked, changing the subject.

Liz smiled at the thought of her father. "He's loving it. I think Florida is doing wonders for his health in retirement."

Noah grinned. "Not to mention the merry widows."

Allison laughed and Quentin managed to quirk a lip.

Liz feigned annoyance. Her father had been alone way too long. If he did meet someone down in Florida, she'd be more than happy for him. "Not Dad. He'd rather kiss a fish."

"I bet he had a great time fishing over Memorial Day weekend," Allison said.

Liz smiled. "You're probably right. He had a big trip planned, but I haven't spoken to him in a week."

She felt three pairs of interested eyes and could have bitten off her tongue. She'd all but admitted she hadn't had the courage to tell her father about her medical diagnosis.

The rest of dinner passed in a haze for her. They discussed the latest headline cases that Allison's office was working on. And Noah and Quentin got into a discussion of the best way to promote their newest software.

When they emerged from the restaurant after dinner, Allison piped up, "Why don't I ride with Noah? His condo is mere blocks from mine in Downtown." Turning to Quentin, she asked, "You're heading back to Carlyle, aren't you, Quent? You wouldn't mind dropping Liz off, would you?"

Liz expected to hear an immediate protest from Quentin, but was nonplussed to hear him concur. "Sure, no problem." He gave her a sardonic smile.

Oh, my. She was in trouble. Noah bent over to give her a peck on the cheek. "I'll catch up with you when I get back." To his brother, he added, "Can I trust you with sweetness here?"

Quentin gave his brother a bland look. Something significant and unidentifiable passed between them and led Noah to chuckle before turning away.

All too soon she was alone with Quentin, whose sure and capable hand at the small of her back led her to a black BMW the valet had just driven up. "Buckle up" was all he said before they pulled away.

They drove in silence. Ominous silence, in Liz's opinion. Like the calm before the storm.

The inside of the car seemed too intimate a space, with the dark pressing around them and Quentin in the driver's seat.

She glanced at him from the corner of her eye. He was looking straight ahead, apparently focused on the road. She wondered what he was thinking.

Of course tonight must have looked exactly like what it wasn't, but she had a logical explanation. Unfortunately, she didn't have the courage to give it without prompting, and he wasn't giving her any encouragement at all.

As they neared Carlyle, she gave him directions to her house. He parked in her drive, helped her out and escorted her to the door.

She fumbled in her clutch for the key and managed to get the door open. "W-well, thank you for din—"

"Invite me in."

It wasn't a request, it was a demand. She nodded and he followed her in, closing the door with a click of the lock.

Three

———

Her house, Quentin took mental note, suited Elizabeth. The first floor, or the front part of it at least, obviously functioned as her office. Victorian furniture with brocade cushions adorned the room. Vintage teddy bears perched on a small corner table and a quilt covered a mahogany rocking chair in another corner.

Feminine. Maternal. Elizabeth.

She started walking toward the back of the house. "Coffee or tea?"

No, just you, please.

Now where the hell had that unbidden thought come from? He was here to make sure she understood that Noah was off-limits to her. And the sooner she understood that, the better. "What the heck were you doing with my brother?"

She halted and turned to face him. "We were having a business meeting.'' Her tone was cool, but her heightened color betrayed her.

He moved toward her. ''Stay away from Noah. He's not potential daddy material.''

She belatedly recognized the threat that his approach posed and feinted to the left. He was faster, however, and moved to the right and caught her, his hands gripping her upper arms. ''Last week you were setting your sights on me.''

''A mere momentary lapse, I assure you,'' she bit back, trying to shrug him off.

''Am I passé already?'' She smelled of lavender and felt even more fragile in his arms than that purple flower. Her movements were also bringing the tips of her breasts in contact with his chest. How horrified would she be to discover that her actions were having the unintended effect of arousing him? ''What if I said I was too hasty in turning you down?''

''Too late.''

''Don't you think you're being a little rash? I'm a much better catch than Noah.''

''Y-you...'' she spluttered.

''But I like to do a little research before closing a deal.'' One kiss. That's all, he promised himself, bending his head.

''You promised Noah you could be trusted,'' she gasped, her heart beginning to race.

''Did I?'' he murmured. ''I don't think one little kiss is a problem, do you?''

She tried to focus on why one little kiss would be a problem, but she drew a blank, her mind turning to mush.

His lips as they settled on hers felt firm, smooth, soft. They teased her lips, rubbing and coaxing, focused on eliciting a response.

She breathed in his warm male scent, felt the gentle scrape against her skin of the evening shadow covering his jaw. His lips moved over hers, urging her to respond, not with a command but with a sweet persuasion that had a languorous warmth seeping through her bones.

How many times had she fantasized about kissing Quentin? About him kissing her? About how he would be? About how they would be together?

And with that thought, she realized that she didn't want to think. She wanted to feel, to savor the moment.

She broke his loose hold on her arms and twined them around his neck and, this time, when he asked for a response, she parted her lips and allowed him to penetrate her mouth, kissing him back with all the pent-up ardor that she thought she'd locked away forever years ago.

She sensed him hesitate for a moment, as if her response caught him by surprise, and then he made a satisfied sound deep in his throat and brought her closer, so that she was flush against him, his arms molding her to him.

Her nipples puckered against his chest, where she could feel the steady beat of his heart. But instead of flushing with embarrassment, as she normally would have, she moaned and sought to get even closer to his warmth, his strength.

His mouth was hot on hers, their kissing taking on a greater urgency.

The reality of him was so much more overwhelming than anything she'd been able to imagine.

She was so lost in their kiss that the ringing sound didn't immediately penetrate to her clouded mind. Only when he groaned and set her away from him did she realize that the phone was ringing.

Her gaze connected with his and she read the blatant desire there. He looked ready to devour her whole!

Flustered, she looked around for her purse. Spotting it on a chair where she'd deposited it on the way in, she pulled out her cell phone.

"H-h-hello?" She cursed her wobbly voice.

"Hey, Lizzie." Allison's voice sounded from her compact folding phone. "I think I forgot my sweater in the back seat of Quentin's car. Can you check for me?"

Darn. How was she supposed to answer? "Er, hold on." She placed her hand over the receiver, and turned to Quentin, who had his hands shoved in his pockets, and looked like a lurking tiger. "Ally thinks she left her sweater in the back seat."

Quentin muttered something unintelligible. "I'll call her from my phone." He headed for the door, turning back when he reached it. "We'll finish this conversation later."

Taking her hand from the phone, she said, "Ally—"

"Can't find it? I could've sworn—"

"Quentin says he'll call you from his phone. He's looking now."

"What?" Allison's voice rose suspiciously. "Where are you guys?"

"Home. I mean, I am. Quentin just left."

There was a definite pause. "I'll catch up with you soon," Allison said quickly. "I think that's Quentin calling now."

Liz slumped into a chair. There was no way she and Quentin were going to finish what they started.

Thank God Allison had called!

After all these years of treating her like a pesky kid, it would figure the darn man would start paying attention just when she was facing her greatest crisis.

Not that he was truly interested in her, she reminded herself. He just didn't want her near his brothers. Because he didn't approve of sperm donations. And beyond that, he might have been curious enough to kiss her.

But that was all.

She bit her lip. She needed the Whittaker account, particularly now, when she might have to take a maternity leave and temporarily shut down Precious Bundles. On the other hand, dealing with Quentin was like handling a lighted stick of dynamite.

Her only choice was to avoid him as much as possible. On Tuesday she had an appointment at a reputable fertility clinic and sperm bank in Boston. The sooner she got pregnant, the sooner Quentin would know how ridiculous it was for him to think she'd seduce Matt or Noah.

* * *

Quentin swirled the Merlot in his glass for the umpteenth time and tried to focus on the conversation happening around him.

Usually he was a natural at these charitable social events. BookSmart was holding its annual black-tie dinner—a fund-raiser for adult literacy—in the ballroom of the Stoneridge Hotel.

He should have been in his element. His eyes drifted again to the woman across the room. He guessed he shouldn't be surprised that the enterprising Elizabeth Donovan was donating her time to raising literacy. And it figured she'd be shimmering in a satiny green strapless dress and matching heels.

As if the woman didn't glow already. Long waves of chestnut locks caught the light as she bent her head toward Eric Lazarus.

Quentin's eyes narrowed. Lazarus. They were about the same age and height but he liked to think the similarities ended there. If anyone deserved the reputation of a womanizing playboy, it was the young stockbroker.

The guy had had the federal Securities and Exchange Commission sniffing around him a while back. Too bad, they hadn't come up with anything. Rumors of Lazarus skating at the edge of the law had swirled for years.

The lights blinked in the lobby where the crowd stood, and the doors to the large ballroom opened, revealing dozens of elaborately set tables.

Lazarus was helping Elizabeth into her seat when Quentin arrived at the table he'd also been designated to be seated at for dinner.

"Lazarus," he acknowledged with the barest dip of his head.

The man's eyes flickered before a practiced smile reached his lips. "Quentin. Good to see you."

Lazarus would pant and roll over for a chance to invest for Whittaker Enterprises. Quentin wondered which would hold the greater appeal this evening: Elizabeth's beauty or his money. His lips twisted as he settled into the chair on Elizabeth's left, Lazarus having already staked a claim to the one on the right.

Up close, he noticed that her strapless gown showcased a large expanse of flawless skin, her collarbone defining her bare neck, which was framed by thick, curling auburn locks that cascaded down her back. He wondered what it would feel like to bury his hands in that thick mass....

"I didn't realize you'd be here," he said, breaking the silence.

She turned to face him, her face impassive. "There are lots of empty seats left." She nodded to the other side of the table, and the room in general.

He refused to take the bait and ignored her uncharacteristic rudeness. "This one suits me fine."

He figured it was at least understandable that she'd be miffed at him. Not that he'd been unreasonable at her house on Friday night. When it came to potential fortune hunters, particularly those with strong reasons to need a financial bailout, he'd learned the hard way you couldn't be too careful.

Of course, he'd interrogated Noah, who'd set the record straight about his "date" with Elizabeth. His brother had exhibited no small amount of amusement at the questioning, but he'd found out enough to know the dinner had come about at Noah's instigation.

On the other hand, despite Noah's persistence, he'd refused to disclose what had happened after he'd driven off with Elizabeth. It was bad enough that Allison knew he'd been in Elizabeth's house that night. There was no point in letting them know just how badly he'd acted.

Which meant, he supposed, that he owed Elizabeth an apology. Given that she was pointedly turned away from him and conversing with Lazarus, he knew it wasn't going to be an easy one to give.

Elizabeth smoothed her napkin in her lap. "No, I haven't been to that new Italian restaurant. I've heard it's wonderful."

"Well, I'll just have to see about changing that," Lazarus said smoothly.

Quentin muttered a curse. If he had to jump in, there was no time like the present. "Business doing well these days, I gather."

Lazarus homed in, a gleam in his eyes. "Never better. I've got a little pre-IPO pharmaceutical company that's just a gem. I can't sell enough shares, if you know what I mean."

"Oh, I do," Quentin murmured. Sounded just like the type of super-speculative investment that a slick salesman like Lazarus would be peddling. "Sounds interesting."

Next to him Elizabeth nibbled at her dinner salad and focused her gaze on the animated stockbroker.

"Interesting isn't the word." Eric warmed to his subject. "We're talking major medical breakthrough

for Alzheimer's here. As soon as the FDA approves
this drug, this baby is going to go through the roof.''

Eric reached inside his tux jacket and pulled out a
business card. ''You know, Quent, you and I go way
back. That's why I want you to get on the ground
floor of the next best thing.''

Quentin took the proffered card. Of course he'd
have to burn it the second he got near a match.

By the time the main course of filet mignon was
served, he knew Elizabeth had to make conversation
with him. The head of the charity was sitting at their
table, and it wouldn't do for the newest board member—as he'd recently discovered—to be rude to one
of the major benefactors. Whittaker Enterprises had
given well into the seven figures to BookSmart.

From the corner of his eye, he watched her first
grimace and then paste a determined smile on her face
before turning to him. ''I didn't realize you were so
involved with BookSmart.''

He forced himself to hide his amusement. ''Philan-
thropy is a hobby of mine.''

''Charity is a labor of mine.''

''Touché,'' he murmured. ''And how do you de-
vote your time, Elizabeth?''

''I tutor people in English.'' She sipped from her
water, and then returned sweetly, ''And how do you
spend your money, Quentin?''

The corners of his lips lifted. ''I write a check with
lots of zeroes so these people,'' he nodded to those
around him, ''can fund libraries and buy books.''

If she was surprised at his forthrightness, she didn't
show it.

"I hope our newest board member is doing her best to persuade you that we do great work here, Quentin," boomed Lloyd Manning, the President of BookSmart, from the other side of the table. "We want you to know how much we appreciate and need your help."

"Elizabeth's made it clear I play a key role." He shot a look at her embarrassed face. "She'll be a charming and effective fund-raiser."

Lazarus took that opportunity to ask Elizabeth to dance. As he watched them move together across the floor, he acknowledged that she'd grown up from the shy teenager she'd been when they'd met.

His mind went back to that day and the demure eighteen-year-old with a shy and winsome smile. At least that's how she'd looked when he'd come trotting down the stairs of his parents' house and had stopped in the foyer where his mother was greeting what he took to be another of Allison's friends.

Allison made the introductions. "Liz, my brother Quentin. Back oh-so-briefly from making waves at Harvard Business School to torture his kid sister over Christmas break. He had nothing better to do."

He looked for the first time into green eyes set in a perfect oval face. Five-seven or -eight, he guessed, with legs that went on forever beneath beige khaki shorts. She'd already been curvy then.

For sure, she would be breaking hearts among the high school boys.

That thought brought him up short. High school. This was his little sister's playmate. Annoyed with himself, he asked, "Liz? Is that short for something?"

"My name is Elizabeth. Liz is a nickname that my father gave me, and it's stuck," she answered.

It figured she'd have a seductive voice, too. He nodded toward his sister. "Are you Allison's play date for the afternoon?"

"I think they've made it out of the playroom, Quentin," Ava Whittaker interjected reprovingly.

"Nice to meet you, Elizabeth," he'd said before heading out the door. Because the more formal-sounding name had seemed to provide a little protection from her attractions, he'd grasped it like a life-saver.

He watched Elizabeth dance with Eric. Years had passed since their first meeting, but she was still wrong for him in every way. She wanted a father for her baby, and he wanted a no-strings affair. She'd been hired by Whittaker Enterprises, and he was the boss with a don't-mix-business-with-pleasure policy. She was his baby sister's best friend, while he said goodbye to lovers and moved on.

Eric's hand moved lower, dangerously close to covering Elizabeth's rear as they danced. Quentin unbent his six-foot-two frame from his chair and strode toward the couple. He could rationalize later.

Quentin clamped a hand on the shorter man's shoulder. "Sorry to cut in, Lazarus." He steered Elizabeth away before Eric could recover. Looking down into her lovely face, he knew that sorry was the last emotion he was feeling. "You can thank me later."

"Thank you?" Color rose to her face. "Why in the world would I thank you?"

"He was pawing you."

"So you saved me so I could be pawed by you instead?"

He laughed. "You seemed to enjoy it last time."

She pursed her lips. "You flatter yourself."

He sobered a little. "Lazarus is a snake. I wouldn't take what he was offering even if he was giving it away."

"Oh, I don't know. A freebie is hard to resist."

His brows drew together. "Don't tell me Lazarus is a potential candidate."

Green eyes met gray. "Okay, I won't."

Her cool attitude irked him, but he refused to be drawn in. "Listen, Elizabeth, I don't know what your current plans are, but Lazarus is bad news."

She sighed. "Eric's an acquaintance. I've made an appointment with a fertility clinic that also has a sperm bank."

He should have been mollified by that, but the mention of a sperm bank set his teeth on edge again. He needed to steer the conversation to safer territory and figured now was as good a time to apologize as any.

He cleared his throat. "I apologize for what I said on Friday night. I jumped to conclusions. Noah set me straight." He was *not* going to apologize for the kiss. It wouldn't have rung true anyway.

She'd been looking over his shoulder, but now her eyes jumped back to his. She looked startled, but then seemed to collect herself. "I—"

He cocked his head to the side. "—accept my apology?" he finished for her, when she seemed at a loss.

She nodded and a small smile played at her lips. "Yes."

He felt relief wash over him, and wondered why her response had been so important to him. "Let's start over."

She nodded, seeming to accept his offer to wipe the slate clean. "I'm sorry I was so rude earlier."

He shrugged. "No offense taken. You had a right to be ticked off at me. Anyway, money is my contribution. I'm too busy to volunteer much time. The fact that you're able to is impressive."

They lapsed into silence then, swaying to some Big Band tune as he guided her across the floor. She felt good in his arms, just relaxed enough to be guided by the subtle pressure of his hand on her lower back.

He enjoyed holding her like this, her body lightly brushing his as they danced. She was close enough that he could breathe in the soft, flowery scent of her. Close enough that he could, if he wanted to, brush his lips across her temple and the curling wisps of hair lying there.

"You dance well," he commented.

"You're surprised."

He thought for a second. "No," he said slowly. "It was just an observation. I knew you'd dance well. It fits with the overall package."

"Oh? And what might that be?"

His lips itched. "You're magnolias and cream with afternoon tea on the verandah." His voice dipped. "Lace and white roses. Incense with delicate spice. A Victorian lady in a rock 'n' roll age."

Liz told herself she should be careful. Quentin's

voice was having a lulling effect on her. "What tipped you off?" she asked lightly, teasingly. "The Victorian rocking chair? Or the brocade furniture?"

He smiled. "That helped. Your house says a lot about you."

"You have me at a disadvantage there."

His eyes gleamed. "That's easy enough to correct."

Liz realized he was teasing her, but still her heart jumped. "No, thank you. I have other plans."

She felt hot all over, not really sure how to handle this "new" Quentin, and said breathlessly, "The music's stopped."

Quentin reluctantly let Elizabeth go and followed her back to their table, where Lazarus had zeroed in on Lloyd Manning. When Elizabeth excused herself, Quentin settled back into his seat.

There were things about Elizabeth that touched him deeply. Always had. On some level, he mused, he'd known and refused to acknowledge it. That's why he'd avoided her all those years ago.

Now she'd grown, matured, and if anything her siren song was even more seductive for him. Her movements, her voice, her lovely face, they all called to him. But even more than that, he recognized her cool reserve for what it was. A front, nothing more. Just like his own professional demeanor.

If their similarities held true, underneath the cool reserve, Elizabeth was a passionate, giving woman. He'd already seen glimpses of it in her uncharacteristic sarcasm at the barbecue, and, God knew, in her response to his kiss.

His experience with women told him that he and Elizabeth were a combustible mix. One that he'd enjoy exploring and testing—if there weren't strings attached.

She'd turned down his offer, as he knew she would. He'd been joking—or told himself he was—when he'd invited her to his house. He'd wanted to establish some of the lightheartedness she had in his relationships with his brothers. But he'd also been disappointed.

Because the bottom line was he wanted her. That's why he'd reacted so strongly to her news about the sperm bank. That's why he'd growled at his brothers.

He took a sip of his wine. Yep. That was it. But just how far was he willing to go to have her? Disturbingly, right now he didn't have an answer.

Four

Returning from the fertility clinic on Tuesday afternoon, Liz pulled up in front of her home on a tree-shaded block in the northeastern section of Carlyle and immediately noticed the black BMW.

Could it be—?

Before she could finish the thought, Quentin came striding around the corner of the house.

Her mind ran through the day-care project. She still had two days to get a more detailed plan to Noah.

Her eyes connected with Quentin's, and he stopped for a split second before striding toward her car. She accepted the hand he offered to assist her out of the car, steeling herself for the usual tingle along her nerve endings.

"I've been waiting for you."

"I see." She concentrated on keeping her voice even. "What can I do for you?"

She'd started for her front door and he'd fallen into step beside her.

"Allison asked me to stop off and pick up the decorations that you have for her cocktail party tomorrow night."

She'd designed small candle and dried flower arrangements for Allison's party tomorrow night for her coworkers. Her usual florist had dropped them off that morning. "I thought Allison was swinging by tonight for those."

He followed her into the house and loosened his tie. "Nope. She had an emergency court appearance this morning. She'll be burning the midnight oil tonight."

"Poor Ally."

"She called me a little while ago, knew I was in Carlyle and heading to Boston later. Asked if I could bring her the stuff."

He loomed in her office, making the space seem small. She tried not to think about the last time he was here. "I'll get the boxes for you," she said quickly.

"So where were you this morning?" he asked while she went through the boxes lying beside her desk.

She felt her face heat and cursed her Irish complexion for the umpteenth time. Too many years of Girl Scout training got the best of her however, and she heard herself say, "If you must know, since everybody seems to know my business these days, I had my appointment at the fertility clinic.''

"How'd it go?''

"Fine.''

"Think it's going to work for you?''

"Yes.'' She straightened and smiled brightly at him. He had his hands shoved in his trouser pockets and an inscrutable look on his face.

She nodded at the five white boxes she'd separated from the rest and stacked beside her desk. "Well, here they are. I'll help you put them in the car.''

"Right.'' He strode toward her, and she took a step back, feeling the edge of her desk at her backside. Any hope that he hadn't noticed her involuntary reaction was quickly dashed however.

Stopping so close she had to tilt her head back, he asked, "What's the matter, Elizabeth? Have you been thinking about what I said the other night?''

"About donating money to BookSmart?'' She shook her head. "I don't collect the money personally. Contact the public relations office.''

He smiled. "No, the other night when we got back here to your house. You know what I mean.''

"No, I don't have any idea what you mean.''

"Liar.''

"Are we going to engage in name-calling again?'' The air between them was heavy and charged.

He bent towards her. "Why don't we kiss and make up instead?''

His arms came around her and his lips captured her mouth. She knew she should stop him, but somehow that thought quickly became lost in the swirl of feelings rising inside her.

He rubbed gently, softly, against her mouth, then caught her bottom lip between his lips and sucked. Whereas his first kiss had been all deliberate seduction, this was a more subtle assailing of her senses, a more quiet awakening of her needs.

She felt hot and aroused, sensations curling through her, urging her to cast off inhibitions. When his tongue entered the warmth of her mouth, she met him, stroke for stroke, fueling the heat.

She'd never experienced these heady feelings with another man. And certainly not with a mere kiss!

She felt a pulsating warmth that coursed through her with a slow, deep, mounting intensity. His hands roamed up and down her back, caressing and molding, and she moaned, her hand coming up to the back of his head, urging him closer.

Abruptly, Quentin pulled back. Breathing deeply, he shot her a penetrating look. "Don't tell me you haven't thought about that. We were on fire there."

She looked at him uncomprehendingly for a moment, before she came back to reality with a thump. She shivered in automatic reaction to the loss of contact with the warmth radiating from him, and wrapped her arms around herself.

Well, of course she'd thought about it! For years she'd thought about it. Imagined it. But it was useless. Right now they could offer each other nothing—except the truce they'd called the other night at the charity event. Just as it had always been, their timing was off.

Her chin came up. "What if I did think about it? It doesn't mean anything. We want different things, Quentin."

His jaw tightened. "Not really."

"What?"

He raked his hand through his hair. "I've been thinking about what you said. You know, about needing to find someone fast and that being impractical, so artificial insemination being the next best thing."

"Yes?"

He slanted her a look she couldn't read. "You said four dates, one month, was the minimum amount of time before you'd consider marriage." He paused. "I can deal with that time frame."

Her breath caught. "What do you mean?"

"Surprised that you don't have a lock on shock value, Elizabeth?"

"No, it's just…I mean…" She gave up on trying to form a complete sentence and wrung out a strangled "I don't understand."

"Let's just say I think Allison may have hit on something."

"That may be a first. You and Allison agreeing."

He gave her a surprised look, nodded and then grinned for a second. "Just don't ever let her know. She'll never let me live it down." He sobered and his gray eyes connected with hers. "I want kids. You want kids. We're both prepared to do some unorthodox things to get them."

"But…"

He took a few steps away from her and then turned

back to face her. His charcoal suit, obviously custom-made, did nothing to disguise the male power beneath.

"I know what I said the day of the barbecue. What I meant was I had no intention of producing grandkids just so my mother can play grandma. I haven't been looking to become a father." His gaze raked her. "But I'm a businessman and I'd be a fool to turn down a good deal."

A good deal. That's what she'd been reduced to. A little flame died inside of her. She hated herself when she heard herself say, "What sort of deal?"

He shoved his hands in his trouser pockets again. "Have you thought about how you're going to manage with this baby? You've got a new business that needs all of your attention. That's a full-time job in itself."

"I'll manage. This is the twenty-first century."

"Precious Bundles has been in business, what? Two or three years? My guess is that your balance sheet is still not looking rosy—" he paused "—or rather, that it is."

Liz flushed. "That's about to change." Precious Bundles was still operating in the red. Most new businesses, she knew, failed within two years, unable to make the critical leap to ongoing profitability.

"What? With the construction of the day-care center at Whittaker Enterprises? Then what? The baby'll be due right around the time you'll need to land another big project. And who is going to hire a business whose sole creative power will be about to give birth, and will be out of commission for a while?"

Much as she hated to admit it, even to herself, he

was right. She was so close to making the business a success, and paying off her small business loan. She just needed a little more time—time she didn't have now.

Quentin was regarding her intently, seemingly able to read the flitting emotions on her face.

He walked over to her rose print couch and sat on the back of it, his legs stretched out ahead of him. "Look, I don't want to depress or scare you."

She gave him a skeptical look. "Really?" she said with a sarcasm that would have made Allison proud.

"Yes, Elizabeth," he said quietly.

Why did he have to call her Elizabeth in that quiet way just when she was building defenses against him?

"We're two adults who are attracted to each other. You want a baby." He blew out a breath. "And I eventually want kids, too."

"Eventually?"

"Yeah, it's not something that's been on my mind a whole lot. I haven't been planning on getting married. At least, not the traditional love-and-happily-ever-after variety."

"Because of Vanessa?"

His eyes narrowed at the mention of his ex-fiancée. "You could say that."

Quentin's engagement had been called off seven years ago just before the wedding. Quentin had remained closemouthed about it all. Not even Allison knew what really had happened.

Liz had been guiltily relieved when the wedding was cancelled. Although she'd met Vanessa at several social occasions, she hadn't really known her.

She forced herself to point out the obvious. "You don't have to be married to have kids."

"In my book you do."

He was making her insides clench nervously. "What are you saying, Quentin?"

"I'm saying, let's give it a shot. Four dates. At the end of it, we decide whether we like each other enough to get married and have a kid together. Right away."

The suggestion was shocking. Clinical, business-like, devoid of emotion, but shocking nonetheless. "Don't you want to marry someone you love?" she blurted.

"I told you, I'm done with that. Elizabeth, I'm a very wealthy man. I don't have any illusions about how the vast majority of women see me."

She looked at him sitting on the back of her sofa, six-foot-two of prime manhood with looks that would make even her oldest clients swoon. Was the man crazy? "And how do you think the vast majority of women see you?"

"As a checkbook," he said curtly, then went on, "what I'm offering here is not the love-and-romance stuff, but something better."

"Better?" she echoed.

He pushed away from the sofa and started pacing. "Yes, better. You get peace of mind and the baby you want. Financial support to make sure the baby is always well cared for and to make sure Precious Bundles stays afloat until you can focus on it again. As for me, my parents will get the grandchild they've been pining for, and which they think it's my duty to produce. Legitimately.''

''What happens after the baby is born?''

''That'll be up to us. We could stay married.'' He shrugged. ''Our arrangement wouldn't be so different from those of lots of other couples at the country club.''

His cynicism ran deep, Liz realized and wondered yet again what had happened with Vanessa. ''Would that be part of the bargain? I'd entertain your clients and executives and dine with the other trophy wives at the country club?''

''No.'' He shook his head in disgust. ''I don't even belong to the Carlyle Country Club. I hate that crowd. But the type of marriage we're thinking about wouldn't be unusual for them.'' He gave her a sardonic look. ''And no, I wouldn't expect you to entertain for me. Just don't expect me to like changing diapers.''

She gave him a droll look. ''What about the fact that I'm still employed by you? Won't people start talking?''

He shrugged. ''The day-care center will be finished soon. And as long as we're discreet, it's nobody's business. I'll admit I have a rule of not mixing business and pleasure—'' he paused ''—but rules are meant to be broken in the right circumstances.''

As crazy as it sounded, the whole scheme was starting to make sense to her. ''And we'd—'' she searched for a delicate word even as her face heated ''—have a baby the old-fashioned way?''

He gave her a sudden lopsided grin. "Or die trying."

She nearly choked. Just how much trying was he planning on doing?

His eyes caught hers, and he asked provocatively, "What's the matter? Do you want me to demonstrate again that we're a combustible mix?"

Automatically she raised her hand to ward him off. "No!" She collected herself and said less stridently, "No, another demonstration isn't necessary."

His eyes gleamed. "I'll pick you up Saturday at eight."

"Where are we going?"

"Leave that to me. I'll call."

And with that he was out the door with the boxes and Liz felt the oxygen in the room again.

By late Saturday afternoon, Liz was running out of things to do to quell her nerves and keep her mind off her looming date with Quentin that night.

When the phone rang, it was a welcome relief. "Hello."

"Hello, sweet pea."

Her face bloomed into a wide smile. "Dad!"

"So! You haven't forgotten the voice of your dear ol' Dad? Thanks be for small favors!" Her father answered in his booming Irish brogue.

"Now, Dad, I just spoke with you."

"And when might that have been, I ask you? Why, a week from Wednesday last, if it isn't a day!"

Wisely deciding to change the topic of conversation, she inquired, "How's the fishing down in the Florida Keys? Still good?"

"Aye, couldn't be better. Caught a bass as big as anything you've ever seen." Her father sighed contentedly. They chatted about his trip a bit and then he asked, as she knew he would, "How's my little girl?"

"Working hard."

"Not too hard I hope. How's about looking to give your dear ol' Dad some pitter-patter of little feet to chase after?"

"Dad!" Her mind drifted to Quentin and she yanked it back.

"Don't 'Dad' me. I worry about you."

Liz sighed in exasperation. Quentin wasn't the only one getting parental pressure. Unfortunately, her father didn't know what a painful topic babies had become. She tried for a lighthearted approach. "If and when I decide to give you 'little feet' to chase, I'll let you know."

"Ah, you're a hard one, lass."

"Goodbye, Dad."

Liz sighed. Ever since her mother had died when she was eight, it had been just her and her Dad. He'd loved her mother Siobhan and had been devastated by her loss. He had had to be both mother and father to her.

And there was the source of the one complaint she could have about her father. He was too overprotective, treating her still as "his little girl."

Naturally, he had tried to convince her to move to Florida when he had retired down there. But she had already started her professional career in Carlyle and had been reluctant to move. She'd also been quietly chagrined that he'd sold his construction business at retirement without even asking if she'd been interested in taking over the company. Sometimes she wondered if things would have been different if her father had had a son.

Elizabeth's house was quiet when Quentin pulled up on Saturday night. He'd dressed in black trousers and an open-collar gray shirt with matching blazer. Reservations at Casa Vittoria in nearby Prescott, the new restaurant Lazarus had mentioned the other night. He derived grim satisfaction from knowing he'd outmaneuvered the stockbroker.

He'd been pumping Allison for information about Elizabeth when his sister had suggested in exasperation that he find out for himself by picking up some party decorations that Elizabeth had done for her.

The more he thought it over, the more he realized that Allison might have had a brilliant idea after all. Frankly, life had started to bore him. The endless procession of Vanessas, each of whom saw him as Mr. Moneybags.

His mouth twisted in memory. Seven years had passed since he'd been a lovesick twenty-nine-year-old entrepreneur on the fast track. So taken in by a pair of wide blue eyes that he'd been deaf to the discreet warnings that family and friends had tried to send his way until it was almost too late.

There'd been an engagement party of course. An expensive dinner affair that Vanessa had insisted on holding at the poshest country club in town. "But darling, everyone makes their engagement announcement at the Bridgewater,'' she had pouted when he'd voiced some doubts about the necessity of the whole thing.

Towards the end of the evening, he'd ducked outside to one of the many terraces to nurse a drink of scotch. Vanessa and her close friend Mara had stopped to chat in the hall inside.

''Vanessa dear, I'm so happy for you!'' Mara had said in her cultured but squeaky voice.

''Thank you, darling.''

''The Whittakers, my goodness!'' Mara had fanned herself with her napkin. It was clear she'd had more than a couple of drinks. ''Why, many are predicting Quentin will be worth over half a billion by the time he's thirty-five! How ever will you manage to spend all that money?''

Vanessa's tinkling laugh had sounded then. ''Oh, Mar, how can you ask that? Have you ever known me to live below my budget?''

Mara had pretended to consider that question. ''Well, *no*.''

They had both laughed like two conspirators sharing an inside joke.

''And just in the nick of time, too,'' Mara had gone on. ''You're so lucky to have reeled in Quentin just as the last money in your trust fund disappeared.''

''Not luck darling,'' Vanessa had said, winking. ''Just playing my cards right.''

''Is poor André brokenhearted?'' Mara asked with a giggle.

''But that's the best part, darling. Quentin is a

workaholic *bore,* but that leaves me plenty of time to continue to recreate with darling André.''

His face had drained of color. The portals to his heart had slammed shut at that instant, and he'd padlocked them for good measure.

The ironic thing was, now even work had ceased to matter as much. And wouldn't Vanessa get a kick out of knowing that?

Sure he still worked damn hard. He just wasn't as driven as he used to be. That fire-in-the-belly, ruthless, single-minded determination to succeed had started to fail him. If ambition were a fire, he'd gone from being a coal-burning furnace to a gas fireplace: all the blaze, but no real heat.

At thirty-six, he realized he wasn't getting any younger. A few months back, one of his chief competitors had up and died at the office from a heart attack. The guy had burned out at the ripe old age of thirty-nine. Since then, he'd caught himself being pensive at odd moments.

So maybe it was time for new challenges. And Elizabeth was that, he thought. She'd demanded a lot, more than he was willing to give. But he'd hit on a plan that would suit them both. A brief period of dating and if all went well, a marriage built on practical considerations.

He'd have her, and the kid he'd almost given up on after Vanessa had cured him of that love-and-marriage garbage. Elizabeth would get her baby and peace of mind.

It was perfect. Brilliant. And he was going to make

damn sure he wrung every second of satisfaction out of it.

Starting right now.

The minute she opened her door, he saw red. Deep, rich wine red. On a dress that hugged her curves in a warm embrace. With a halter-top that exposed her creamy shoulders and graceful neck.

He cleared his throat. "Here." He handed the flowers to her. "For you."

"Th-thank you." She bent her head to sniff the fragrance of roses mixed with lilies.

He followed her into the house. "You're welcome."

"Lilies are my favorite."

"They match the color of your dress." Great line, Whittaker.

"Make yourself comfortable. I'm just going to put these in water before we go," she called over her shoulder.

He'd watched her sashay to the kitchen. If anything, the back view of her in that slinky dress was even more arresting than the front one.

She came back with the flowers arranged in a glass vase that she set on an end table. "Would you like something to drink?"

"No. Let's get going." He sounded more brusque than he'd intended, and she looked taken aback.

The truth was he didn't trust himself in the house with her. Her toenails, he'd noticed, were painted a deep red and peeked out from strappy, high-heeled sandals. The effect was unbelievably erotic.

After she'd gathered a black sequined purse that he

swore could hold no more than a set of keys, and a fringed shawl, he followed her out the door.

Casa Vittoria was a quarter of an hour away on a road he knew well, so they reached the restaurant in what seemed like record time.

They were seated at one of the best tables in the house and Quentin made a mental note to thank his secretary Celine for seeing to it. Immediately a waiter appeared to offer them menus and the wine list, while another filled their water glasses. The first waiter recited the specials of the day in accented English.

Quentin looked up in surprise from the wine list when he heard Elizabeth ask a few questions in seemingly flawless Italian. When the waiters had departed, he asked, "Where did you learn Italian?"

A smile touched Elizabeth's lips. "College. I minored in Romance languages. After my mother died, Dad and I vacationed abroad a lot. I guess it was his way of trying to compensate for my mother being gone. By the time I got to college, I loved French, Italian, Spanish." She'd been turning the stem of her water glass as she spoke and now groped to steady it as it almost tipped over.

Ah, Quentin thought with satisfaction, at least she felt a little of the tension he'd been feeling since he'd first laid eyes on her this evening. Emboldened, he reached out and removed her hand from the glass to trace slow circles on the back of her palm. "Careful," he murmured.

The soothing motion of his index finger on her hand sent a languid warmth through Liz, even as she felt caught and trapped by Quentin's intense gaze. His eyes had turned a deep slate-gray and she wondered idly if she'd ever seen that shade before.

Only the arrival of the waiter to inquire about their wine selection saved her. She quickly withdrew her hand and tried to steady her breath, thankful that Quentin had been distracted.

"I thought I'd order a Chardonnay," Quentin said with a telltale twinkle in his eye, and Liz realized he was teasing her about her partiality to the wine.

"Mmm, that would be wonderful." She took a sip from her water glass as Quentin ordered an old vintage. Seeking a neutral topic, she said, "Allison says you've been very busy lately."

She hadn't said a word to Allison about her "dates" with Quentin. It would get Ally's hopes up prematurely.

Quentin sighed and leaned back in his chair. "Yup. I'll be traveling most of next week."

"You don't seem happy."

He gave her a tired grin and for the first time she noticed he looked a little peaked. "Living out of a suitcase is never fun."

"But you have to do a lot of it."

He nodded. "More than I'd like. The computer world is a mile a minute. And a lot of our business partners are based in California. What about you?"

"Most of my clients are based in Massachusetts. There's a fair amount of travel, but it's local."

The waiter returned to take their order and when he departed again, Quentin asked, "Have you thought about how you're going to handle that when you've got a kid?"

The directness of the question threw her, and she looked at him startled. He shrugged. "It's come up at work. We have part-time, flex-time and work-at-home arrangements for our employees."

"That's admirable."

His lips quirked in that telltale way she associated with his sardonic half smiles. "The truth is that if I hadn't thought it was good company policy, my mother and Allison would have had my hide."

She tried not to laugh. "I'm sure your employees thank you."

He arched a brow. "Actually the biggest dividend was getting on the cover of Parent-Child magazine over the caption 'Trailblazing Cutey-Pie CEO Is Big Hit with Both Wall Street and *Sesame Street* Crowds.'"

She laughed delightedly and he joined in.

"Worse things have been said about you," she offered.

He nodded. "Yeah, that's true. Expect the worst and get pleasantly surprised."

"Oh, is that your motto?"

"One of many," he parried.

"And the others would be—?"

"Today's dreams are built on yesterday's reality."

She cocked her head. "Hmm, never heard that one before."

He motioned away with the glass in his hand. "Made it up."

"Ah," she sighed, "a closet philosopher."

He raised an eyebrow. "The Victorian lady meets Machiavelli?"

"Is that who you are? The realist philosopher who thinks the worst of human nature?"

He leaned forward. "Every entrepreneur is partly Machiavellian. Comes with the territory. Don't let anyone tell you differently."

"Meaning I'm just masquerading as a demure and proper Victorian lady?" she asked, guessing that Precious Bundles qualified her as an entrepreneur.

His gaze perused her and then he grinned unexpectedly. "No," he rejoined, "that's just one side of you. Another is the bottom-line businesswoman. Otherwise, when I offered you my deal, you'd have slapped my face and cut me dead."

He was dissecting her unerringly. "Perhaps I've just decided to play along."

He shook his head. "Nope. You play for keeps."

A shiver went down her back. Playing for keeps was exactly what they were doing, and the stakes were never greater.

Five

When they arrived back at her place, she invited him in for tea, and, after a brief pause, he made a sound that seemed like a yes and followed her in.

Inviting him in was the most nonchalant move. She was desperate to have him think she was able to handle their dates with cool aplomb.

She thought of his past dates. How had she compared? She'd done her best tonight to fit his type. She looked down at her dress as she poured water into her floral tea kettle. The dress had been an impulse buy yesterday. Afterwards, she'd stopped in at Louise's Spa and Salon for a matching naughty red pedicure.

Yes, she looked a little vampy. And it had required every inch of nerve she possessed to try to pull off that look tonight.

She'd wanted to attract Quentin of course. But another part of her had also wanted to shock him—make him see her as a bold, daring woman who was comfortable with her sex appeal. She'd been pleased when she'd opened her front door to him tonight and seen his eyes widen.

She set the kettle to boil and started arranging some of her homemade pecan chocolate chip cookies on a platter. She always baked when she was nervous, as she had been before their date this afternoon.

Now if only she could pull off the rest of the evening without making a cake of herself. She looked down at the platter. Too bad she hadn't thought of baking a cake instead to guard against that urge.

When she came back into the living room with her laden tea tray, Quentin was fingering the lace tablecloth covering one of her end tables. "Antique?"

"My mother's," she said as she set down her tray on the coffee table. "It's a McConnell family heirloom. Just like most of the antiques I own."

He sat down on the hump-backed sofa beside her. Liz was grateful the sofa was firm and straight-backed, in the Victorian style. Anything else would have made sitting within a hair's breadth of Quentin unbelievably intimate.

"Tell me about your mother."

"There's not much to tell." She sighed. "She died when I was eight. She had an inoperable tumor."

"I'm sorry," he said deeply.

The look in his eyes was one she'd never received before: sympathy mixed with respect. "I have some memories of her. Sometimes when I see gardenias I'll remember her flower arrangements, or when I smell split pea soup, I'll remember her cooking dinner.''

"How old was she when she died?"

"Only twenty-nine."

"The same age you are now."

He'd obviously drawn conclusions about the connection between her mother's death and her own need and desire to have a child as soon as possible. "Yes, but I'm going to win my battle."

He nodded. "Growing up without a mother can't have been any fun, but you succeeded anyway."

She cleared her throat and looked away quickly. Compliments were not something she accepted comfortably. "Th-thank you," she managed.

She was, Quentin thought, a delicate flower with a strong stem. Her straight back and thrust-back shoulders would have impressed the finest etiquette teacher. The clean lines of her oval face were full of delicacy and strength at the same time.

When she'd invited him in, he'd hesitated. The two of them alone in her house would present a temptation that was hard to resist.

But he'd figured she'd just misinterpret him if he declined her polite offer of tea, just as she'd obviously misinterpreted his abruptness when he'd picked her up at the beginning of the evening.

When the truth was the woman was bringing him to a slow boil. All that fire covered by a cool veneer was enough to drive any guy crazy. Especially one with a newly discovered taste for a chestnut-haired interior designer with a honeyed voice and a peaches-and-cream complexion.

A heaviness settled beneath his belt. Damn. He cleared his throat. "Tea looks good. Going to pour us some?"

"Oh, yes." She was embarrassed to discover she'd forgotten to serve the tea.

Great, Liz. She chalked up another strike against the cool and sophisticated image she'd wanted to project tonight.

She brushed his knee as she poured tea, and tried to ignore the quiver that went through her. She determinedly picked up a cookie. If she was going to be sinful, better that it be with food.

She went still as Quentin picked up a strand of her hair, eyed it idly, and then proceeded to twist the end of it around his finger.

"Cookie?" she offered.

He chuckled. "Sure." He paused. "I seem to have my hands full—" he nodded at the hand that still had hold of her long hair "—so why don't you feed it to me?"

"I, umm...."

"Here, I'll give you a hand," he said, then bent forward to take a healthy bite out of the cookie still in her paralyzed hand.

Oh, my. She felt nervous and languorous at once. How was that possible?

He bent forward for another bite and took the remainder of the cookie out of her hand.

"I hope you like pecan chocolate chip," she said inanely.

He swallowed. "I do. I hope you do, too."

"Oh, they're my favorite."

He nodded thoughtfully. "That's good. Very good."

"Why?"

"Because I'm going to kiss you and it will be a whole lot more enjoyable if you like the taste of pecan chocolate chip."

"Oh!"

And that was the last she got to say before he let go of her strand of hair, turned her toward him, and took possession of her mouth.

The first time he'd kissed her had been a masterful seduction. The second had been gentle persuasion.

This was sheer bliss. He seemed familiar now with how to touch her. Seamlessly, they moved together from gentle nibble to the deep, soul-searching quest of mouth on mouth.

Liz shuddered. Her hands moved through his hair, bringing him closer, seeking more of the pleasure he gave, the sexual knowledge he possessed, the comforting familiarity he harbored.

Quentin's brain clouded. He'd intended to give her only a light, teasing kiss tonight, to ease their way into a more intimate relationship. He'd underestimated their need, their desperate desire for each other. The one or two kisses they'd shared up till now had done nothing to dampen that.

The sweet lavender scent of her seduced his senses. Her skin was so soft and smooth, he had an uncontrollable desire to touch it, expose more of it.

His hand propped up her chin to deepen the kiss, then touched the side of her face before wandering to stroke her arm, her midriff, the line of her hip.

He urged her backward until she felt the arm of the sofa under her head. Her mind clouded as his lips left hers to run a line of moist kisses across her soft cheek, nibble at her earlobe, and then trail down her neck.

She shifted restlessly.

"Shh," he coaxed. "Easy. Nice and slow and easy."

He sounded more in control than he felt. His hand shook slightly as he unclasped the back of her halter-top dress.

Lord, but she had a powerful effect on him. He wondered now how he'd been able to keep his hands off her for so long. Frankly, if he'd had any idea of how easily she'd be able to get under his skin, he didn't think he'd have had a hope in hell of staying away from her.

Her eyes flew open when he eased the dress and its built-in support from her, exposing her breasts.

He looked into her incredible golden green eyes. "Beautiful." His voice sounded hoarse with desire. Reverently, he reached out and caressed her breasts.

Liz closed her eyes again. The feel of his hands—strong and slightly callused against her nipples—was incredible.

When his mouth replaced his hands, she jerked at the unexpectedness of it and then shuddered with pleasure. She tangled her fingers in his hair, holding him to her. The steady, rhythmic pressure of his mouth sent waves of electric sensation through her.

Just when she thought she couldn't bear it any longer, however, he moved to the other breast, replacing his hand at the first, where the nipple was now wet and distended from his attention.

Again he brought her to the brink. When she thought she couldn't bear his attention any longer, his lips finally came back to hers. Mouths met, hands roamed, bodies shifted. She wanted him so much. Why wait?

And with that thought, she pushed until his jacket came off his shoulders and down his arms and then set to work on the buttons of his shirt.

He lifted his mouth from hers and gave a husky chuckle, looking down at his suit jacket bunched around his wrists.

"Please…" She felt as if she'd only been dreaming of the possibilities up till now and he'd awakened her to real emotion, real sensation, real desire.

Leaning back, he finished off his jacket and shirt with a couple of quick, efficient movements. He was lean with strong shoulders and fine ebony hair on his chest. She trailed her fingertips over him and his eyes closed, seeming to savor the moment. Then he raised her hands above her head and leaned back down toward her.

Cold replaced by hot. Lips replacing air. His hands and mouth played over her body.

She felt the evidence of his need for her and instinctively reached down between their bodies to touch him.

Groaning, he pressed himself into her palm for a moment and then tore his mouth from hers and sat back.

His eyes were hot, his breathing a bit labored.

Her first instinct was to sit up and press her mouth to his and move his hands back to her breasts, where they could continue to do wonderful, wicked things to her. But then she read the look in his eyes. The look that said, stop me now or I won't be able to stop at all.

As he reached out to pull up her dress to cover her, realization dawned about how far they'd gone—and how fast.

She felt herself redden, embarrassed because he'd been the one to stop. She moved to get her dress back on without revealing her breasts again, refusing to look at Quentin—which was ridiculous really, since he was sitting on the sofa, right next to her, half dressed.

"Do you need a hand?" he asked, his voice deep and still a little thick from the effects of their love-making.

"I believe your hands are what, ahh, caused this predicament to begin with," she muttered half to herself, still refusing to meet his gaze.

He held his offending hands out in front of him. "Okay, guys, now cut it out." He knitted his brows. "How many times do I have to tell you not to wander off?"

She looked up, having hooked the halter-top back into place. "What? Oh." She planted her hands on her hips and decided to play along. Anything, anything to diffuse the situation. "The old the-hands-did-it routine."

He gave her a serious look. "Hanky and Panky apologize."

She tried desperately and unsuccessfully to school her face.

"I'd suggest handcuffs, but they'd just consider that kinky."

A chuckle escaped her.

He gave her an amused look, then picked his shirt up off the floor and stood to shrug into it before grabbing his jacket. Bending, he gave her a firm peck on the lips and filched another cookie. "Thanks for a wonderful evening." He shoved his hands in his pockets and cocked his head toward the door. "Come lock me out, so I'll know you're safe."

The flowers arrived the next day. A dozen, long-stemmed white roses with reddish tips interspersed with lilacs. The note said simply, "Thanks for a special night. Will call soon. Quentin."

The next week passed quickly for Liz.

On Tuesday, she was at Whittaker headquarters to speak with potential contractors for the day care and was almost limp with relief, knowing Quentin was traveling and not in the building.

The brochures from the fertility clinic continued to lie in her desk drawer where she had placed them. They beckoned to her, telling her she was crazy to have even entertained Quentin's scheme.

Allison called on Wednesday. If Quentin had divulged any information, she couldn't tell from Allison's responses.

"We won!" Allison exclaimed over the phone.

"Won?" Had Quentin said something to Ally about their date?

"The trial. The jury came back with a verdict in our favor. Those crooks are going to pay through the nose!"

Liz sighed in relief. The last thing she needed was for Allison to jump the gun and start broadcasting to all-and-sundry that she and Quentin were becoming parents—together. "That's great!"

Allison seemed to come back to earth. "So how have things been in Quentinland?"

"You mean the epicenter of the Whittaker quest to take over the computer world?"

Allison snickered. "You know, Liz, that's why I always thought you and Quentin would be a fantastic match. You'd be the magical antidote to his outsized ego."

"Oh, I don't know. Quentin isn't that bad."

"What? We're talking about the guy who honked and hollered when he picked me up from the prom. The guy who suggested my first boyfriend was one French fry short of a full pack."

Liz chuckled. "You mean, Lenny? Wasn't he the one who accidentally bonded his fingers together with glue?"

"That's beside the point," Allison retorted. "The point is that my brother has been the bane of my existence. And he's so obtuse, he doesn't even know it."

She couldn't resist asking, "Why would you want to pass him off to me then?"

Allison sighed. "I know. It's diabolical of me. But it's the only way I could think of to get rid of him finally." Then added in exasperation, "Now it seems not even you want him."

Liz rolled her eyes. Heaven help her, they were skating on thin ice. She was able to end the call, however, before Allison got any further down that dangerous road.

Allison's call broke some of the restless tension of the week, but by Thursday morning Liz was eyeing the telephone like it could sprout legs and walk away.

With some determination, however, she finally got enough concentration to focus on Mrs. Elfinger's playroom. So when the phone rang, she answered with a distracted, "Hello, Precious Bundles."

"Which one am I talking to?"

She fumbled with the receiver and nearly dropped it. "Which—uh, what?"

"Which precious bundle am I talking to?" Quentin repeated. "You know, that's a very suggestive line. Another guy might not understand."

She colored. "I haven't had any problems so far." Trust Quentin to be able to fluster her even when he was hundreds of miles away.

His chuckle sounded over the line.

"How—how have you been?" she asked, striving for polite conversation.

"Working my butt off. We should have this deal sewn up soon though. We're acquiring a Web site to provide phone-book-type information through Whittaker's portal site."

"Sounds like you're making inroads into the market." Allison had told her when the portal site had been launched three years ago.

"Yeah," Quentin was saying, "but we're just one step ahead of our competitors. We need to stay on it."

She eyed the arrangement of flowers at the edge of the desk. "Thank you for the flowers. The roses and lilacs are still blooming beautifully."

"You're welcome." Was it her imagination, or did his voice drop a notch? "Sorry I didn't call earlier, but we've been on almost a 24/7 schedule here. I've been thinking about you."

She tried for a lighthearted laugh. "Thinking about how many other ways I might try to insult you?"

"Nope, not by a long shot."

A tingly warmth went through her. She didn't want to dwell on what he had been thinking about.

After a pause, he continued, "I'll be back in the office on Monday. Meet me there. We'll have lunch."

"I—I'll be at your offices on Monday anyway to look over the day-care site. The contractor I hired has been tearing down walls."

"Great. Come to my office when you're done. We'll go to lunch from there."

When Liz walked into Quentin's private reception area at noon on Monday, a sprightly sixty-ish woman looked up at her inquiringly.

"I'm here to—"

"—see Quentin," the gray-haired woman finished with a smile, rising and coming around her desk. Liz felt interested eyes sweep her from head to toe. "He's just finishing up a call. Can I get you something to drink, dear?"

"Oh, no, I'm fine, really."

The door on the far wall opened suddenly and Quentin appeared, his suit jacket missing and his hair tousled where he'd obviously been raking his fingers through it.

When he noticed her standing in front of Celine's desk, he stopped abruptly and smiled. "Elizabeth."

She felt foolishly happy at his sudden smile. "Hello, Quentin." She was acutely aware of Celine absorbing everything with great interest.

"I see you've met the incomparable Celine O'Sullivan," he said, amusement in his eyes.

Celine shot him a reproving look. "Now, Quentin, you know I'm just a little ol' secretary trying to put up with you until I can retire and collect that pension you've been promising me."

Quentin just chuckled as if that had been a long-standing joke between them.

Liz wracked her brain. The last time she'd been in Quentin's office, another woman, a temp obviously, had sat behind Celine's desk. "I don't think I've met Ms. O'Sullivan before."

Celine gave her a bright smile. "Just Celine, dear. And no, we haven't met before, though I believe we've spoken by phone."

Celine threw Quentin an amused look that he returned blandly, and Liz realized Celine must have been the woman who had called her to set up that first meeting in Quentin's offices—the one that had ended with the clinch and near kiss downstairs at the site for the day care. Feeling her face heat, she wondered what Celine knew about that initial encounter.

"I've heard so much about you," Celine went on. "You're Ally's friend, aren't you?"

"Yes, I'm Liz."

The phone rang then and Quentin strode back to his office, leaving the door ajar, and calling over his shoulder, "I'll be back in a minute."

Celine's eyes twinkled. "He really is a good man but don't ever tell him I said that."

"The newspapers love him."

"Oh, phooey!" Celine waved a hand. "Quentin would rather pore over business reports than spend time at social functions, which he sees as a necessary evil of his job. The papers love him just because he's young, handsome, rich and eligible."

Celine gave her an encouraging look that nearly made Liz blush. Obviously Quentin's secretary had formed her own opinions and one of them was that Quentin should settle down.

She hated to think of Quentin leading some solitary existence however, so she asked, hoping to change the subject, "But he doesn't just work?"

"Oh, my dear, Quentin was always very intense— and I've known him for years, worked for his father since Quentin was a baby."

Celine looked away, reminiscing. "Everyone knew he was going to do great things. And I don't just mean in business, although goodness knows he's been successful there. I mean, the kindness, too. He's very loyal to those around him." Celine's eyes came back to hers. "Why, the stock that man has gifted to me...well let's just say, I'm not still in this job because I need it."

Liz absorbed the information. If his secretary was to be believed, there was a whole other side of Quentin that a privileged few were allowed to see.

Liz glanced up as Quentin reappeared in the doorway. "Sorry," he said ruefully, "minor emergency with our European operations, so this is going to be a long call."

Liz nodded. "That's no problem at all. It'll just give me a chance to go back down to the day-care site and make some more progress."

"I'll call the restaurant and move back that lunch reservation for you, Quentin."

"Thanks Celine." To Liz, he said, "I'll come find you when I'm done."

When Liz got downstairs, the day-care center was a scene in suspended chaos. The workmen were all on their lunch break. Tools lay scattered amid ladders and buckets on the tarpaulin covering the wood floor.

Liz had been down here during the morning to talk to the contractor, but now she had a chance to take measurements without getting in the way of the construction crew. She pulled a retractable tape measure from her bag along with a pad and pencil and set to work.

After almost an hour she'd taken some measurements, jotted down some notes, and drawn a couple of rough sketches of some details she was considering.

She looked around the open space again. Yes, it was coming along just as she'd envisioned. They'd have an office to one side for the administrators, some

child-size tables and chairs for the kids set up in the
open area in the middle, and play stations to the left
for building with blocks or playing with dolls.

She was still uncertain where to put the cubbyholes
for the kids though. The far wall looked good. But so
did the one on the left. She bit down on the edge of
her pencil, contemplating the options. The wooden,
paint-stained ladder near the far wall caught her eye.

With the ladder, she'd be able to mark off where
the cubbyholes and cabinets would be placed and get
an idea of how it would look.

She decided to try the right wall and walked over
to the ladder. When she set the ladder against the wall,
it was just high enough for her to mark off where the
tops of the cubbyholes and cabinets would be.

Starting at one corner, she climbed up the ladder
and marked off where the cubbyholes would start,
then got down, moved the ladder over, climbed up
again, and marked off some space for cabinets. She'd
set those a little higher, she decided, and break up the
architectural lines a little bit. Given how many kids
there'd be, they might have to have two rows of cubbyholes, one on top of the other.

She moved the ladder over again and made some
additional markings, then took a step down before realizing the end of the wall was within reach.

Taking a step up again and balancing on her beige
sandals, she reached over and marked a spot on the
lower corner of the wall before reaching to do the
upper corner near the ceiling. She was just a couple
of inches short, so she took a step to the side and
leaned over a bit further.

Suddenly the rung of the ladder under her feet gave way and she lost her balance. "Ohh!!"

Rather than hit the floor with a thud, however, she was surprised to find herself caught in a pair of strong arms. The ladder went crashing to the ground, the sound reverberating in the large, empty space.

"Dammit! What the hell were you doing?" Quentin demanded.

She brushed back loose strands of hair from her face. "My job."

"Balanced on top of a ladder with—" he looked disdainfully at her strappy sandals "—Barbie doll footwear?"

"The ladder gave way!"

He nodded grimly toward the ladder with the broken rung now lying sideways on the floor. "Yeah, but that still doesn't explain what in the blazes you were doing on top of it."

If he'd simply been concerned, she'd have reacted differently. Instead, his anger fueled her own temper. "What I was thinking was that I should do my job." She thought a second. "You're paying me to get this day-care center done, and if you're satisfied with the end result, you can keep your opinions to yourself."

It was ridiculous to be having an argument when he still held her in his arms, but she hated being scolded like a child. "Put me down," she said. Then added, "Please."

He hesitated for a second, seeming reluctant, and then lowered her to the floor. The second her right foot hit the ground, she winced.

"What's wrong?" he demanded.

Even if she'd wanted to hide her reaction from him, she couldn't have. The pain shooting out from her foot was strong and sharp. "I think I strained something."

Six

_____

Oh, heck. He picked her up despite her halfhearted protests.

"Be quiet and stop squirming," he grumbled. "You're going to a doctor."

"Well, of course I am—"

He looked down at her and the look in his eyes was enough to silence her. He bent with her and let her pick up her purse.

Damn.

His heart had risen to his throat when he'd seen her teetering on that ladder with those ridiculous sandals and his alarm had made him sound sharp.

Even now his pulse was galloping, except, if he was willing to admit it to himself, it wasn't only because of what had nearly happened. The side of her breast pressed against his chest, her rounded backside within inches of his hand under her legs. He gritted his teeth to tap down the welling of lust.

He strode with her past some gawking messengers and the receptionist, whose look of surprise turned into one of amusement at the sight of her boss carrying a woman in his arms.

"Suzy, call Dr. Grover and tell him I'll be there in fifteen minutes."

"Right away!" The receptionist placed the call, and Quentin could hear her talking to Dr. Grover's office assistant even as he strode through the automatic front doors of the building.

"Put me down! I'm capable of getting myself to the car—"

"How?"

Color rose to her face. "And anyway, I have my own doctor."

"Glad to hear it," he said pleasantly, "but today we're seeing mine."

"You're used to calling the shots, aren't you?" The question was accusatory. "Don't you ever take commands?"

He slanted her a look. "Under the right circumstances…" he murmured, letting the sentence trail off—and was rewarded with another blush.

"Where are we going?" Liz glanced out the car window at the highway exit they were passing, then jerked her head around to Quentin. "You just passed my house."

The doctor they'd seen had told her that her ankle had been badly sprained. While she wouldn't need a cast, she'd have to use crutches for the next couple of weeks.

"We're heading to my place."

"What?" Panic roiled her stomach.

He took his eyes off the road for a second. "Don't worry. I don't have any nefarious schemes in mind."

"Of course not." So what if she'd been thinking just that? "I simply meant, to what do I owe the pleasure of your unexpected and unsolicited invitation to your place of abode?"

He chuckled, then cleared his throat. "You're going to need someone to look after you for a while. I have a great housekeeper. You'll love her."

"Oh, no—"

He tossed her a penetrating look. "Don't even try to argue."

She raised her chin. "I'll be able to manage just fine."

He looked back out at the road. "How? You're supposed to keep off that foot. Do you have anyone at your place to help with cooking meals? Running errands? Getting around the house?"

"I can stay with Allison."

"Forget it." He took his eyes off the road long enough to shoot her a droll look. "You know as well as I do that Allison works late regularly, particularly when she has a trial going on. And, except for the occasional cat-sitter, she doesn't have any household help at her apartment."

He was right, much as she didn't want to admit it.

"Look on the bright side. This will give us a chance to see if we're really compatible."

She felt a little flutter of panic. "What about my things?"

"Not a problem. I'll swing by your place and pick up anything you need." He paused, then added, "Does this mean you accept my invitation?"

She studied his profile until he turned and looked at her blandly. She sighed. "Yes."

She'd seen Quentin's house from the outside of course. She often passed it on trips to meet clients in the most exclusive section of Carlyle. He'd bought it shortly after his engagement.

The wood frame house dated from the mid-1800s. White shingles and a white picket fence set off by black shutters and doors. The two-story structure was partially obscured from the road by two large oaks in the front yard.

She'd often thought it was the sort of house she'd have bought if she could have afforded it. And, she'd often itched to have a look inside, wanting to know if it would be as she'd imagined. But her enthusiasm had been tempered by the knowledge that Quentin had bought it for another woman.

"I'll show you around a little so you have your bearings," he said as soon as they were inside. "I don't keep a big staff here because I'm often traveling. Just a weekly cleaning service and gardener. Fred O'Donnelly and his wife Muriel fill in as the part-time butler and housekeeper."

She admired the alabaster banister on the stairs leading from the foyer, where they were standing, to the level above. The wood shone with a dark-red glow. "Is this the original woodwork in the house?" she asked as she turned to look at the nearby doors and their equally dark wood frames.

"Yes." He opened the door on their left and she used her crutches to hobble into the living room after him. "The fireplaces have also been carefully maintained."

A spectacular marble mantel dominated the room. A couple of mauve couches faced each other across a small coffee table set on a cream mohair rug. "The stuff in this room, and in most of the rest of the house, I moved in from my bachelor pad. I started some of the essential restoration and renovation, and thought I'd leave the decorating to Vanessa—"

He cut himself off and his jaw tightened. "The engagement was over before we got to that point, but then you probably know that, don't you?" He slanted her a look.

"Allison did mention the engagement, yes." She had been living in Carlyle but working for a design firm in Boston at the time. She had dreaded perhaps being hired by the future Mrs. Quentin Whittaker to do the interior decorating for the house. When the engagement had been called off, all the local gossip columns had carried the news. Speculation had run rampant over the cancelled engagement of the scion of the Whittaker clan to the Boston Brahmin society belle.

She used her crutches to maneuver over to the mantel. "It's lovely."

"I'm glad you like it." His voice held a note of quiet pride.

"Who did you hire for the restoration and renovation?"

He mentioned a name she was accustomed to dealing with. "Yes, I know them well. They do great work."

He glanced at her crutches doubtfully. "If you can manage, I'll show you the rest of the house."

"I'd love to see more."

The downstairs was completed by a study, dining room, kitchen and family room. All contained the same lovely woodwork. The spacious kitchen contained all the modern amenities, though its traditional style made it harmonious with the rest of the house.

"The kitchen had just been redone when I bought the house," Quentin offered as they moved to the stairs.

"Mmm." She was distracted by her surroundings, or she would have noticed his pause as they reached the bottom of the stairs.

"I'd better carry you."

"Oh, that's not necessary...." So far, being held in his arms hadn't failed to send her pulse racing. "I can manage these steps just fine—"

"Yeah," he took the crutches from her suddenly nerveless fingers, "but I can't manage to just stand back and watch you," he replied in a smooth voice.

Before she knew it, she was swung up into strong arms and held close to a broad muscled chest. If she'd forgotten anything from her encounter earlier that day with certain parts of Quentin's anatomy, this was a great reminder! "Put me—"

"—down," he finished for her. "No. Now stop fidgeting."

His warm breath disturbed some tendrils of hair at her temples. With her arm around his neck and her hand holding his far shoulder, she felt his muscles flex and move as he effortlessly carried her up the stairs.

She focused her gaze at his collarbone and bit her lip. The temptation to kiss along his jawline, just shadowed with stubble, was disturbing.

When they mercifully reached the second floor, he put her down, being careful to support her with one hand until she'd had a chance to plant the crutches he handed back to her.

She cleared her throat. "Thanks."

"You're welcome."

The second floor had five bedrooms, and two were not furnished at all, she soon discovered.

"I haven't had a chance to do anything about those," he said almost apologetically. "It's been years since I bought the place, but I've let the decorating sort of languish."

They paused outside the third door. "This is the master bedroom," he said as he opened the door.

She wasn't sure what she'd been expecting, but it wasn't the sight that greeted her. Antique furniture in a rich rosewood filled the room, which was dominated by a king-sized bed. Cream-colored bedding, upholstery, and drapes offered a sharp contrast to the wood finish. The result was breathtaking.

Quentin liked antiques? And if looks were anything to judge by, he was fairly knowledgeable. She was impressed. She was, no, stunned. "This was in your apartment?"

He grinned at her shocked tone. "Hey, don't sound so surprised. The word 'taste' and I are not completely incompatible."

"Sorry, it's just I pictured something…er…."

"—with leather and lots of mirrors?" he supplied with a chuckle.

An involuntary smile rose to her lips. Embarrassed that he'd been able to guess her thoughts, she changed the subject. "I had no idea you liked antiques."

"At Harvard, I'd sometimes go for a drive to take a break from cramming for exams. Occasionally I'd come across an antique show, or just someone's yard sale."

"I'm just surprised because you didn't seem to give any thought to the decor in your office," she offered.

"True. But that's not personal space, it's work space. I figured those guys at the architectural firm knew what they were doing. I sure paid them enough."

She picked up the clock on the bureau. Its elaborate woodwork marked it as a Victorian-era piece. "This is just charming."

"I have a great collection of clocks and time-pieces," he said as he came up to stand next to her.

"I suppose the watch museum in Geneva is your favorite museum?" she teased.

"You've been there?" He looked surprised. "I've visited several times, when I can spare time on a business trip."

"Yes, I visited it on a trip to Europe during college."

"This furniture I picked up through an antiques dealer. Except for the bed frame. That I bid on anonymously at an auction."

"Yes, it's impressive." She went over to the bed and gave it an obligatory pat. "Do you know the age?"

"Dates from the 1890s."

"Did you need to restore it?" He had walked up behind her as she skimmed her fingertips over the headboard.

"No, it had been kept in great shape."

"That's good." She was very aware of him and the tension coiling within her. Trying to keep the conversation going, she went on, "Intricately hand carved, I see."

"Yup." Was it her overly-sensitized senses, or had the timbre of his voice deepened a notch? She kept her gaze focused on the headboard.

"Must have been expensive." He was very close now, his breath disturbing her hair, and blocking her means of escape.

"Yeah, but I liked the intricate carving."

His hand settled over hers on the headboard, guiding the tip of her index finger over the swirling indentations and protrusions of the smooth wood.

Oh, boy. She was melting like butter in the sun with the heat emanating from him. Her gaze fixed on his hand covering hers, unable to look away or slip her hand from his as he continued to move their hands over the headboard.

"You can tell he took his time," he said huskily. "Everything needed to be perfect, and so he created something astoundingly beautiful."

Just when she thought she couldn't stand any more, he dropped his hand from where it covered hers. Before she could exhale however, his hands settled on her shoulders and he nuzzled her neck.

She struggled to keep her voice even. "Perhaps the craftsman didn't work alone."

He turned her to face him. He was smiling, his eyes crinkling in amusement. "You think?"

"As an expert on antiques, I can assure you, he didn't."

"How can you be sure?"

"Great work is often revealed to be the result of a great collaboration," she managed to say before his head dipped for a kiss.

"Maybe he was a hermit."

"And creating a beautiful headboard big enough for a king-sized bed?" she asked skeptically.

He chuckled. "Hmm, good point." His lips trailed kisses from her brow down to her jaw. He removed one of her crutches and dropped it on the bed, replacing its support with his arm around her waist. "Maybe he just liked big beds."

It was getting harder and harder to concentrate on their conversation. "He must have had someone to inspire him."

His fingers fumbled at the zipper of her sleeveless top. "Honey, you're inspiring me right now."

Only when cool air greeted her back did she realize he must have lowered the zipper on her top to allow himself better access. His hand came up to cup her breast over her sagging top and he allowed his thumb to trace around the outer edge of the nipple before peeling the top away from her.

She heard his swift intake of breath and met his hooded gaze. "Do you have any idea what you do to me?" he asked huskily. He lowered his eyes again to her breasts, which strained against the wisp of fabric that was now their only protection against his heated gaze.

Then all coherent thought was lost as he bent his head and his mouth closed over one tight nipple through the lacy fabric of her bra. He began to suck, his tongue moving over the peak again and again.

Liz moaned and distantly heard her remaining crutch hit the carpet with a thud. Her hands moved to hold his bent head to her breast. His arms now were her only support as he transferred his ministrations to her other breast.

She thought she would die from the pleasure of it. The gentle sucking was causing a myriad of exquisite sensations to course through her and settle at the juncture of her thighs.

"Quentin, oh, please…"

Only the two of them and their overpowering need for each other seemed to matter.

He deposited her on the bed and came down on top of her. His kiss was all hot and hungry male passion.

His hands were everywhere, caressing, stroking, smoothing, stoking her passion. Her bra was disposed of and her breasts lay against his hair-roughened chest. The friction, coupled with the feel of his erection at the juncture of her thighs, caused the tension to coil ever tighter within her.

He sat up quickly, and though she felt momentarily bereft, she was glad to see him shrug out of his suit jacket and then divest himself of his shirt and tie.

His chest was covered in a T of curly hair that tapered down and disappeared into the waistband of his pants, which could not hide his erection.

Her gaze lingered for a second before rising up to meet his eyes. The passion reflected there caused her breath to catch.

She'd wanted him, wanted this, seemingly forever. She raised her arms to him but he shook his head.

"No, not yet," he murmured. "First let's get you out of these." He unbuttoned her pants and peeled them from her, panties and all, careful not to jolt her injured ankle.

She felt vulnerable, exposed, lying there before him, without an item of clothing to hide any of her flaws. She lay still, waiting for his reaction and was surprised by his slightly crooked grin.

Trailing his eyes from her hips up to her face, he explained, "Your hair is the same color *all over*. I was curious about that."

She felt the heat rise to her face even as he chuckled and came down beside her, his leg urging hers apart. His hand cupped her intimately before he used two fingers to begin a swirling motion against her hot center. Slowly and deliberately he built an ache of pleasure until she squirmed on the bed for release.

"Quentin!" she gasped.

"I want to hear you say 'yes,'" he reproached on

a laughing groan. "Can you say it for me, sweetheart?
I want to hear you say it."

Coherent thought was impossible. Never had she
felt so sensual.

"Give yourself to me," he rasped.

His supplication was Liz's undoing. She went spinning into oblivion. "Oh, yes! Yes! Please, Quentin!"
He made a guttural sound of satisfaction at her climax.

After her gaze refocused, he came up over her.
"We're not finished yet, honey. Not by a long shot."

Just as he bent his head and positioned himself to
enter her, they both heard it. The unmistakable sound
of the front door opening, followed by a called-out
"Hallo-o? Quentin?"

The breath hissed out of Quentin as he slumped on
top of her, collapsing in seeming defeat. "Damn,
damn, damn."

Liz tried to clear her head. "Who—?"

"Muriel. The housekeeper," Quentin's muffled
voice announced grimly from the pillow next to her.

"Oh. Ohh!!" Liz struggled to sit up. "Oh, my."

Quentin lifted his head and gripped Elizabeth's
arms to stop her from struggling. "I'm upstairs, Muriel," he shouted. "I'll be down in a minute." Then
he levered himself off of her, generously giving her a
hand so she could sit up.

Her gaze took in his muscled, still aroused body.
The man was flat-out gorgeous.

"Stop giving me those looks, sweetheart. Otherwise, we'll finish what we started, Muriel or no Muriel."

She felt the stain of a blush and quickly looked

about the bed for any item of clothing within her reach.

"Here." He held her bra and panties in his fist. "They were on the floor."

"Thank you." Then with as much dignity as she could muster, she took her underwear from him.

"Victoria's Secret black satin. I would never have pegged you," he said, pulling on his trousers.

She felt her blush deepen. "Stop it," she muttered. She envied the way he'd rapidly collected himself when they'd been interrupted.

He sat down on the bed next to her, his still unbuttoned shirt gaping open, and lifted her chin so that she was forced to meet his gaze. "You have the most fascinating blush." He glanced down. "It starts amazingly far down."

She pulled her chin away. "Irish blood. Some of us aren't blessed with a poker face."

He grinned. "Thank God for that."

She jumped when he bent and placed a moist kiss at the center of her cleavage.

He winked, looking devilish. "Just wanted to see if it feels as hot as it looks."

She grabbed a pillow and aimed for his laughing face, but he grabbed it before it could reach its mark. "Get dressed. I'll stall Muriel and be back in a minute to help you downstairs."

As soon as he was gone, Liz tried to make herself as presentable as possible. She ran a brush through her hair and applied some lipstick. Her clothes were a little mussed, but they'd have to do.

She mulled over what had just happened—or

rather, what hadn't, thanks to Muriel's fortuitous interruption. She'd been angry with Quentin's high-handedness when they'd left the doctor's office. Yet, a short time later, she'd been rolling on his bed with him.

She had to be careful and guard her emotions. Quentin had made it clear that theirs would be a union based on practicalities and that's just the way he wanted it. If she didn't remember that, she'd be in trouble.

Muriel turned out to be a pleasant, plump-faced woman around sixty with steel-gray hair and glasses hanging from a chain around her neck.

"Allison sent you over," Quentin repeated slowly.

"Why, yes, dear," Muriel said. "She called me about an hour ago. Said she'd heard Liz had had a fall and you'd taken her to your doctor. When the doctor told her you'd mentioned on the way out that you were taking Liz home to keep an eye on her, she called me straight off."

Liz caught Quentin's droll look and bit her inner cheek to keep from laughing.

"Yes, indeed," Muriel continued. "She suggested I might want to come on over to see if someone was needed to look after Liz." Muriel placed her hand over her heart. "In a bit of a muddle, aren't we?"

Quentin had his suspicions about his sister, but decided to keep quiet about them for now. "A muddle all right." And he knew exactly which of his siblings was responsible. He scratched the back of his head.

Muriel gave him a beatific smile. Celine's bridge

partner knew how to play it fast and sly. He'd bet
against the house that Muriel was in cahoots with his
sister. "I'm going to go back to work. On the way
home, I'll pick up some things for Elizabeth from her
house."

Muriel clasped her hands. "Splendid idea." She
walked over to Elizabeth, balanced on crutches, and
began to lead her to a kitchen chair. "Why don't I fix
us some cool iced tea, hmm? Then we can set you up
with a phone and fax and anything else you need in
Quentin's study."

Seven

"**I** have Mother Teresa at the house, her bridge partner at the office, and the Whittaker Women's Patrol every place else," Quentin said morosely.

Matt snickered.

"At least Fred's not spying on you through the bushes," Noah offered.

They were at Earl's having a couple of beers at the bar, as they sometimes did on those rare days when all three brothers had no plans and weren't busy at work.

It was welcome relief for Quentin. Elizabeth had been camped out at his house for over a week. During that time, his mother, his sister Celine and Muriel had conspired to make sure he wasn't able to have a free moment alone in Elizabeth's company.

"Frankly, I'm surprised," Matt said quietly. He

nursed his beer, arms resting on the bar, gray eyes surveying the bottles lined up in front of the mirror on the back counter. "Is it just the weather that's got you all hot and bothered, Quent, or something else?"

Quentin nudged Noah on his other side. "You think he speaks in tongues?"

Noah gave a lopsided grin. "Naw. We probably knocked loose a few too many marbles when we used to kick his butt."

"Selective memory, little brother," Matt retorted. He took a good gulp of his beer. "Let me spell it out for you two clowns. Muriel, Celine, Allison and Mom all existed in your life last week, Quent. And the week before that, and the week before that. Why are you so worked up about it now? What's different about this week?"

"Matt," Quentin said slowly, as if talking to a child, "Muriel is camped out at my house."

"Mmm-hmm." Matt cracked open a peanut. "So I hear."

"She's up in the morning making fluffy pancakes when I get down to the kitchen, and downstairs watching *Murder, She Wrote* reruns when I go to bed at night. The woman never sleeps!"

"She naps in the afternoon when you're at the office," Noah offered helpfully.

"Damn straight." Quentin signaled for another beer. "Allison calls every night." Just when he thought he'd have a few moments alone with Elizabeth, his sister would call. He'd be treated to peals of laughter and snatches of a one-sided conversation that would go on and on.

"Oh, man," Noah commiserated.

Quentin thought he'd had them last Saturday, Muriel's bridge night, but then Allison had shown up with pizza.

He'd practically wrung his hands with glee on Monday when Muriel had reluctantly announced she and Fred needed to attend a church meeting. But then his mother had called and asked him to stop by on the way home from work to pick up some books that she wanted to give Elizabeth. Of course, the whole thing had turned into a two-hour detour and by the time he'd gotten home, Elizabeth had been asleep.

He didn't kid himself that he understood women, but after nearly thirty years with Allison, he'd started to understand some of the devious paths her mind ran down. She and his mother—along with Muriel—were running interference for Elizabeth. Their suspicions had been awakened about his current relationship with Elizabeth, and although they couldn't know about the "deal" that had been struck, they suspected enough about his motives to believe that Elizabeth needed some protecting. And he wouldn't put it past Allison to have decided that having Elizabeth so close yet so unattainable was exactly the sort of lure he needed.

"Keeping Liz under lock and key, huh?" Noah asked, pulling him back from his thoughts.

"It's unbelievable," Quentin said, then caught himself and shrugged. "It's all the same to me." Except it wasn't.

"Your bad mood wouldn't have anything to do with Lizzie, would it, bro?" Matt arched a brow.

Quentin hadn't told his brothers about his "arrangement'' with Elizabeth. They knew something was going on, they'd just uncharacteristically avoided probing. Anyway, how did he explain that he might father Elizabeth's baby after the negative reaction he'd had to the possibility they'd do the same?

Quentin shook his head. ''She hasn't bothered me.''

Like hell. Sure she hadn't intruded on him, but her mere presence in his house was driving him crazy. Knowing she was down the hall—maybe in that lacy negligee he'd retrieved from her house for her—was enough to make it hard to get to sleep.

''Great.'' Noah exchanged a look with Matt. ''Then you won't mind her puttering around the house all weekend under the same roof.''

''Shut up.'' Quentin sighed. He wasn't fooling anybody.

''Monday is the Fourth of July,'' Matt said matter-of-factly.

Quentin took another swig of beer. ''Think she'd like to sit on the grass, listen to the Boston Pops and watch the fireworks?'' he asked morosely.

''Women love that kind of stuff,'' Matt said.

''Can't go wrong,'' Noah seconded. ''Pack a picnic basket. And don't forget the Chardonnay.''

''Great.'' Quentin felt some of the tension ease from his neck and rolled his shoulders. He thought his instincts were right, but it was good to know that Matt and Noah agreed.

Noah tossed some bills on the counter. ''Gotta run.''

''Noah,'' Quentin stopped his brother.

"Yeah?"

"If you or Allison 'coincidentally' shows up at the concert on Monday, I'd have to kill you."

Noah grinned. "I'll pass that warning along."

Saturday night. Unbelievably Muriel had left around eight, saying Fred needed her help installing some shelves.

Right, thought Quentin. As if he'd fall for that ruse. He wondered what the "plan" was now. Had the dogs been called off? Had Noah relayed his message of the night before to Allison, and had his sister finally seen fit to give him some breathing space?

Well, he wasn't falling for it.

Think they could make him dance like a puppet on a string, did they? So, he was alone in the house with Elizabeth. That didn't mean he'd start pawing her at the first opportunity.

She was holed up in his study, doing work. Fine. He'd cede his work space to her for the evening.

He'd just make himself comfortable on the couch, get a cold beer and watch the Boston Red Sox play while he looked at the latest status reports from various departments at work.

It was the bottom of the fourth and still no runs when the phone rang. Dropping the report he was reading, he reached for the cordless on the end table. "Hello?"

"Oh, Quentin,…hi."

"Don't sound so surprised, Allison. This is still my house."

"Of course I wasn't surprised, Quent. Don't be

silly.'' Allison paused. ''It's just that I thought Lizzie would pick up. I've gotten used to calling her over there.''

Quentin crossed his legs on the coffee table. It was payback time. ''Your timing's off.''

''What do you mean? Is Liz there? Pass her along, hmm?''

''I mean, you're too early to interrupt us *in flagrante delicto*.'' He glanced at his watch. ''Call back in an hour or so.''

''Quentin!'' Allison exclaimed.

''Bye, Ally.''

''Quentin, wait! Quentin?''

''You've got five seconds.''

''Okay, you're onto me.'' Allison sighed dramatically. ''What do you want? Should I engage in self-castigation? Promise I'll never hatch another devious scheme?''

''Don't make promises you can't keep.''

''All right, all right. But remember, big brother, you're there alone with Liz and I'll expect my trust to be repaid.''

''Contrary to popular belief, I'm neither a depraved animal nor an ogre,'' Quentin said dryly. ''I've even heard some women have confessed to liking me. 'Charming' and 'gentlemanly,' I believe, were the words used.'' He paused. ''On the other hand, that could just be a vicious rumor.''

Allison laughed. ''You of all people shouldn't believe gossip!''

''Yeah,'' he conceded.

"Just remember what I said," Allison replied before hanging up.

Quentin replaced the receiver, shaking his head. He got up to get himself some chips to go with the beer.

It was ironic. Here he was, parked in front of the television on a Saturday night, alone with his beer and chips. He shook his head. He led a far more boring life than most people—including his family, it seemed, and not to mention, Elizabeth—believed.

He picked up the discarded report from the couch and scanned it. Settling back he began to read.

Half an hour later, he'd digested most of the report and searched for last month's report from the same manager. The only way to get a good picture was to put things in historical context.

He searched his briefcase with no luck. It was probably on top of his desk. In the study.

He paused in the doorway to the room where he usually worked at his desk. The yellow light cast by the lamp failed to reach the shadows at the edges of the room.

Elizabeth sat in the easy chair, reading. Unobserved, he studied her. Her hair was up, pinned in a loose knot, some tendrils escaping and caressing her face. Tortoise-rimmed glasses perched on the edge of her nose, a slight frown betraying her concentration.

She looked adorable and Quentin was unprepared for the tenderness he felt. He stuffed his hands in his pockets. "Don't you know that frowning causes lines?"

She glanced up. "You startled me!"

"Sorry." He made his way into the room. "I just came to find the report I'm missing."

Remembering the glasses, Liz quickly took them off. She hardly ever got caught wearing them. It helped that she was only slightly farsighted.

"Don't take them off on my account," Quentin said in an amused voice.

She reached for her eyeglass case, embarrassed he'd read her actions. "I guess you've discovered my dark secret. Are you going to tell your brothers that Liz Donovan is the mousy librarian sort that you took her for all along?"

He glanced back at her and stopped rifling through the papers on his desk. "It's a good thing you took them off—"

She knew how she looked, but did he have to spell it out for her?

"—because I think women in glasses are very sexy."

Her eyes shot to his face.

"I see I've surprised you. Again."

She thought about what her reaction had been to seeing his bedroom for the first time and felt heat rise on her face.

He removed a stapled-together set of papers from a pile. "Finally."

"I'm glad you found the report."

He walked over and sat himself in an armchair nearby. "Aren't you going to ask me why?"

She pretended to pick a piece of lint off her khaki shorts. "Why what?"

"Why I think women in glasses are sexy."

"I'm sure you have your reasons," she said politely. She waved a hand. "After all, ah, men seem to discover their 'type' early on."

He leaned forward and braced his arms on his haunches. "I've given this some thought." He turned his head toward her and Liz raised her brows inquiringly. "It's the intelligence that glasses signal."

"Hmm."

"Also, they kind of make a man itch to peel away the layers. What's she hiding? Can she be wild and uninhibited as well as prim and proper? That's the mystery."

She folded her arms. "I see."

"The library was one of my favorite hangouts." He grinned. "All those sexy librarian types hitting the books."

"Sort of like the fox in the henhouse, hmm?"

He sat back and laughed. "Sort of," he said, still grinning.

"What about those women you're always pictured with in the papers? Bambi or whatever?"

"Bambi?" he spluttered, laughing again.

She nodded seriously.

"All right." He held up his hands in mock defeat. "I'll admit I haven't been picky when it comes to my Friday night dates." He shrugged. "I've taken out whoever is around and willing to go to these boring social functions I always seem obligated to attend."

"And 'whoever is around' is the sleek high-society type."

He sighed. "Whether the woman is my type or not

is often beside the point.'' He nodded to the papers she'd set aside. "Work?''

She felt herself smile. "Yes. We bespectacled librarian types spend a lot of Saturday nights alone working.''

The corner of his mouth curled up. "So do we dashing playboy types,'' he admitted. "I'm camped out with my files in front of the TV in the other room.''

"Oh!''

"Why don't you join me?'' He looked around the study. "Work someplace else for a change.''

The offer was tempting, Liz thought. She didn't have a good reason to refuse, so she let him move her things to the other room, hobbling behind on her crutches.

When they had her settled in an armchair, Quentin put the television on mute so that he could keep tabs on the game while he and Elizabeth worked.

"By the way,'' he said, "Monday is the Fourth of July. I thought I'd go to the Boston Pops concert. Care to come?''

He'd sounded so casual, it took Liz a moment to digest what he was saying. She'd wondered in the past few days whether her accident had derailed their four dates and now felt ridiculously pleased that he wasn't abandoning their original plan. Aloud she said simply, "That sounds wonderful.''

They worked in companionable silence for over an hour. It was closing in on nine o'clock when Liz caught herself staring off into space. She removed the glasses she'd put back on in order to work.

"Problems?" Quentin asked.

Liz shook her head. "No, just envisioning what the Lorimers' kitchen would look like in yellows and blues." Her lips curved. "And how to fit in Mrs. Lorimer's request for an island, two sinks, and a built-in cupboard."

Quentin quirked a brow. "Here's my solution—hit Mr. Lorimer up for a bigger house."

Liz laughed. "His wife has already tried that. He doesn't even understand why she wants to do away with the avocado-green appliances."

"A sink is a sink." Quentin sat back on the couch. "Anyway, what's the problem? Didn't bell-bottoms come back into fashion? In a couple of years, the neighbors will be falling over themselves to copy her."

Liz tilted her head to one side. "Ah, I see. Retro-chic."

"Exactly."

She pursed her lips. "Kitchen appliances don't come back into fashion the way clothes do. When was the last time you saw someone trade in their washing machine for a washboard?"

"Yeah, all right, I'll give you that." Quentin eyed the television. Bottom of the ninth and the score was tied.

"Thank you."

"So what about giving her two kitchens. His and hers, maybe."

"That's ridiculous."

Quentin folded his hands behind his head. "Oh, I

don't know. The guy might want to mess around on his own sometime.''

She rolled her eyes. ''I don't think—''

Not taking his eyes from the television, Quentin interrupted, ''Okay, then add onto the house. Does the kitchen share an outer wall?''

''I already thought about that.'' She shook her head. ''They've got a patio in the back and a driveway along the side of the house. I can't expand.''

Quentin took his eyes off the television. ''Get rid of a closet or two. Knock down a couple of walls. Give her a pantry instead of closets. The hubby won't care, he thinks she has too many clothes anyway. And she'll be so taken with the idea of expanding the kitchen, she'll forget about the closets she's losing.''

Liz tapped the eraser-end of a pencil against her lips. ''Hmm, that might work. She does have a couple of closets next to the kitchen.''

''Next year, she can get the husband to go along with the idea of expanding another part of the house to add a walk-in closet. And ta-da,'' Quentin snapped his fingers, ''another project for you!''

To say she was surprised at his insight was an understatement. She supposed she shouldn't be. After all, he'd risen high and fast in the business world. And he really did have a good idea. She started to tell him so when she was caught by the action on the television screen. ''Quick! Raise the volume. I think the Red Sox have scored!''

Quentin scooted forward and grabbed the remote.

''A home run, folks!'' the announcer exclaimed.

"And that's the ball game. Red Sox 4, Orioles 2. We'll be right back after these messages!"

Quentin looked at her. "I didn't know you were paying attention."

"I guess I was doing a better job of hiding it than you were," she shot back.

Quentin grinned. "Sorry. I swear I was paying attention to Mrs. Lorimer's kitchen—too."

Liz folded her arms. "And I was about to tell you that you had a great idea—about the closets, I mean." She paused. "Thanks."

"You're welcome."

They smiled at each other for one inane instant.

They were so comfortable together, Liz thought. Why had it taken them years to reach this point?

And yet, he hadn't confided in her. Not about Vanessa. If they were going to have a baby together, she'd want to know that much about him. He could play his cards close to his chest, but sometimes he'd need to throw one on the table.

"Quentin?"

"Hmm?" he answered, not tearing his eyes from the screen.

He must have figured that if she was onto him, there was no reason for him to hide his divided attention anymore, Liz thought ruefully. She took a deep breath, "What happened between you and Vanessa?"

His eyes shot back to hers. "Pardon?"

"Why did you break off the engagement?"

Quentin looked back at the screen and sighed. "Game over." He flicked off the television with the remote in his hand.

Liz shifted a little in her chair. She would not regret asking him. The worst he could do was tell her it was none of her business.

She hoped he wouldn't. She didn't want the evening—and their newfound camaraderie—to end on a sour note. She didn't want to remember that it was her fault by blurting out the question that had been gnawing at her since…well, since longer than she cared to remember.

He was quiet for an instant. "I found out she didn't love me so much as my money—and the status of being Mrs. Quentin Whittaker."

There, he'd gotten it out. He hadn't told anyone before about the end with Vanessa. Not even his brothers.

He waited for the humiliation to burn. Leave a bitter taste in his mouth. But saying the words, the emotions were a distant echo of what he'd once felt. He figured he'd finally reached the point where he could look back with disappointment and not bitterness.

She nodded. "How are you so sure about Vanessa's motivation? Surely, she didn't come right out and say she was marrying you for your money."

"Don't be too sure," he muttered.

"What?"

"I overheard her and a friend of hers talking. On the balcony, at one of those black-tie affairs that Vanessa loved." He shrugged. "They didn't know I was there."

"I see."

"No, you don't see." He ran his fingers through his hair. "Apparently, I was the fish she managed to reel in before her trust fund money ran out.'' He laughed mirthlessly. ''Vanessa always had expensive tastes.''

''I'm sorry.''

He shook his head. ''There were family and friends who tried to give me a heads-up. But I ignored them.'' He paused and then said reflectively, ''I guess I should consider myself damn lucky it all came out before the wedding.''

Elizabeth bit her lip. ''Surely she must have had some feelings for you.''

Now that he'd started, he figured he might as well tell all. ''She was planning to take up with an old lover of hers after the wedding. Conveniently, my work schedule gave her lots of free time.''

Liz looked at Quentin—all six feet two inches of pure male sprawled on a bottle-green sofa. She couldn't imagine wanting anything—or anybody—else if she had him.

What a horrible blow to his pride it must have been. How humiliating, too, to know that others had known—or at least suspected—even when he hadn't.

''A workaholic bore, she said.'' He grinned unexpectedly. ''Not too far off the mark—'' he cast her a sidelong look ''—even if some people insist on seeing me as a playboy.''

Liz felt herself flush. She could hardly explain her view was due both to finding him very attractive and needing a defense against that attraction.

''Now you know the details.''

''Yes.'' She felt ashamed at her nosiness, but something compelled her to ask, ''How is what we're doing any different? It seems to me that, by the terms of our, ah, agreement, I get to use you for your money.''

''Nothing wrong with that *if* both parties are up-front about it.'' He regarded her levelly. ''Let's just say that, after Vanessa, I've started to think that it's not such a bad deal...*if* the ground rules are established at the beginning.''

''Rather cynical, wouldn't you say?''

He shrugged. ''Look, even if the romance-love thing exists, a lot of us aren't that lucky. A sizable chunk of the world would probably be better off approaching the whole thing like a business deal.''

''I see.'' So that's where his brilliant idea of having a baby together had come from. It was all part-and-parcel of his post-Vanessa philosophy about love and marriage. It had just taken him time to realize she'd presented him with exactly the sort of proposition that he'd come to see as ideal. Except for speeding up the baby stage, it all fit very nicely.

''By the way,'' he said quietly, bringing her back from her thoughts, ''you were wrong when you said you're no different than Vanessa.'' He paused. ''You won't have any lovers on the side. That's part of the deal.''

His steely look nearly took her breath away. Even though she knew it wasn't possessive in the way a man normally felt for a woman, it made her quivery inside.

Eight

They were settled on the Esplanade next to the Charles River in Boston on Monday evening waiting for the Boston Pops to play at their annual Fourth of July concert.

A rectangular red-checked sheet that Muriel had found was set out beneath them. With some help from Muriel in retrieving things, Liz had prepared tarragon chicken salad sandwiches on French baguettes, mesclun and tomato salad with vinaigrette, and apple cobbler for dessert.

Quentin had good-naturedly teased her about the pretentiousness of the mesclun in her salad, and she'd retaliated by poking fun at the age of the Chardonnay that he'd picked out.

Ever since her discovery a couple of nights ago about the deep-seated roots of Quentin's cynicism about women, Liz had been troubled about having bitten off more than she could chew. On the other hand, she figured things were in some ways simpler than she'd thought. There was little chance that Quentin would fall in love and want to marry someone and regret the "deal" he'd entered into with her.

Even if he did, she decided she'd cross that river when she came to it. After all, she and Quentin had yet to agree whether he would try to father her baby. Tonight she was going to enjoy this concert.

A slight breeze teased her hair, but otherwise the evening was balmy and clear. She tugged down the hem of her knee-length, blue cotton dress. "It's wonderful out here."

He looked up at her from behind wire-rimmed sunglasses. He was sprawled on the blanket, his hands behind his head, looking up at the dark evening sky. He radiated relaxation in navy T-shirt and gray khakis. "Haven't you ever come to listen to the Pops on the Fourth?"

She shook her head. "Actually, never. When Dad and I moved to Carlyle, he'd send me back to spend summers with Aunt Kathleen on the Jersey shore. After that, I'd always have the types of summer jobs that got busy on holidays."

"Like what?"

"Oh, you know, baby-sitting, serving ice cream, working at the bike rental shop."

His eyebrows rose. "You worked behind the counter at an ice-cream parlor?"

"Candy-cane-striped apron and all."

His lips quirked. "I can't picture it."

"In college, I was known for the homemade variety," she informed him, pretending to look down her nose.

His smile widened. "Do tell."

He reached for her hand on the blanket and began drawing small circles on the back of her palm, sending a delicious tingle through her. "It's not that complicated to make ice cream. You just mix eggs, sugar, milk and cream. The hardest part is getting the right consistency."

"You learned to cook—"

"Aunt Kathleen. Dad's okay, but I took over most of the cooking by my teens."

He was silent for a moment, his fingers stilling on her hand, and she could feel his gaze through the sunglasses. "You and your father are close." He made it a statement, not a question.

"Yes, but it's a complicated relationship."

He angled his head even as his hand crept up and began stroking her arm. "Is there any other type?" he drawled.

She smiled, momentarily forgetting about that wicked hand. "I tried to be the son that never arrived."

"Ahh." Quentin thought back to what he knew about Patrick Donovan. Big Irishman, owned a small construction company before retiring. They'd had a few business dealings, enough for Quentin to know the man was a shrewd operator.

Liz scanned the crowd, which had thickened in the last half hour. "The silly thing is that my father loved having a daughter." She put her arms behind her and braced herself on her hands, lifting her face to the small breeze. "I was all pink frills and baby dolls. The little girl he needed to protect."

She gazed back down at him. "The only problem was that I felt too protected. I wanted Dad to see me as independent, capable."

Ah, Quentin thought, so that's what made Elizabeth Donovan click. Fascinating. He sat up and removed his sunglasses. "Kind of hard to ask a guy who's lost his wife not to be protective of his little girl."

She sighed and nodded, looking away. "Yes. I've come to understand that."

"Is that where starting your own business came from? Sort of a strike for independence?" he asked, though he already knew the answer.

His perceptiveness surprised her, but she merely nodded in agreement. "Some of it was that. But I was also ready to move on from the big architectural firm. I had my own ideas, and I wasn't getting the chance to realize them."

Why had she revealed so much to him? One minute they were talking about ice cream, the next she was baring her soul.

He raised a finger and traced a line between her brows. "Don't look so worried."

She tried for a game smile. It had been years since she'd taken out these feelings and examined them. It was one thing to think about these things privately, it was another to give voice to them.

As if reading her turbulent thoughts, Quentin stroked her hair and said, "It's all right. All kids have some fears."

She looked at him, so strong, so solid, so seemingly cool and invincible. "Really? What were yours?"

He chuckled. "I guess I opened myself up to that one. Mine was that I wasn't sure I'd be able to fill Dad's shoes with the company." His gentle stroking was soothing her and she nearly purred when he started to massage her scalp. "Even us sons have our worries."

"Hmm."

"I remember your father had a small construction company. Sold it as I recall," he said casually.

She blinked, trying to keep her mind focused on the conversation. "Yes, mmm, he sold it when he retired."

To a larger conglomerate which had subsequently been sold to a holding company that Quentin had formed with some more minor business partners. Quentin realized she didn't know about the relationship between him and the company that her father's old business had eventually been folded into.

Knowing what he knew now, he doubted the information would be welcome to her. And, frankly, he didn't need another strike against him. No doubt, on some level, Elizabeth questioned whether her father would have sold the company if there'd been a son around.

The concert started then—the Pops launching into a rendition of Sousa's "The Stars and Stripes Forever"—and they lapsed into silence.

They had a new connection between them, Liz thought. Forged of newly discovered shared experiences. She hadn't thought it would be so easy to talk

to him, tell him things that she hadn't even revealed
to Allison.

She stole a look at him. They were more alike than
she'd ever imagined. Although, she mused, maybe
she'd always intuitively known about his power to
read her like a book and that had been part of the
tension between them.

There was only one word for a man who made her
feel like he could glimpse her soul: Dangerous.

When they arrived at Quentin's empty house, he
carried her back from the car. She didn't protest as
much as she had in the beginning, though the tingle
of awareness was there every time. It ran through her
from the thousand points where their bodies touched.

He deposited her in the living room. "Coffee," he
suggested.

"Please, let me do it," she said, grabbing her
crutches, which he'd carted in with her. "You can
finish unloading the car."

He hesitated for a second, then nodded and strode
out.

When his back was turned, Liz gave a little smile.
Maybe it was his recent knowledge of how important
her independence was to her, but he'd just stopped
himself from giving orders instead of taking them.

She hummed a little as she reached the coffeepot.
The crutches slowed her down a bit, but the doctor
had said she might be able to get rid of them within
the week.

When Quentin materialized, she let him take the
coffee cups and followed him back into the living

room. He sat right beside her on the couch, the arm of the sofa preventing her from shifting away even if she'd wanted to.

"I enjoyed the concert," she said, suddenly a bit shy. "Thanks for taking me."

"You're welcome." It had been hard keeping his hands off her on the lawn. Now that they were alone, his self-control slipped down another notch.

He searched his brain for suitable conversation. "I've always liked concerts. My mother forced all of us kids to take up an instrument. Mine was the sax." He looked around. "Wonder where Muriel hid the damn thing."

She chuckled. "Hall closet, second door on the right, behind your hockey trophy from high school and an old basketball."

He should have known. "Gave you the grand tour, did she?"

"I'm afraid so." She tried to hide a smile by taking a sip of her coffee. "It happened one day when you were at work."

"Figures."

Elizabeth stifled a yawn with her hand, then rubbed her eyes.

"Tired?" he asked. He moved his hand to rub the nape of her neck, which, he'd come to realize, was an erogenous zone. He looked forward to replacing his hand with his lips soon.

"Mmm." She arched her neck to give him better access. "Quentin?"

"Yes?" Her eyes were closed and he leaned toward

her, intent on trailing his lips along the curve of her long and graceful neck.

"Why do you call me Elizabeth?"

The question caught him off guard and he reversed his forward motion. Heck of a time for her to ask *that*. "Are you sure you want to know?"

She opened her eyes to gaze at him. "Is it really terrible?"

He pretended to contemplate that for a second. "Depends on how you look at it." She looked irresistibly sweet sitting there on his couch. He nearly groaned aloud when she wet her lips.

"I really want to know."

His cover was about to be blown, but there was no help for it. He took a deep breath. "Calling you Elizabeth helped me mentally keep you at a distance." He blew out the breath. "Elizabeth is a lot more formal-sounding than Liz or Lizzie. It reminded me to keep our relationship on a strictly 'hello-goodbye' basis no matter how lovely you were and how attracted I was to you."

Reading the mixture of doubt and surprise on her face, he added ruefully, "You were a threat. I was a twenty-five-year-old guy who found himself in the uncomfortable position of lusting after his little sister's best friend, who wasn't even out of high school." His eyes connected with hers. "Of course I was going to cut you out."

Her brows had drawn together in puzzlement. "I thought you didn't like me. Matt and Noah were friendly, you were—"

"—a jerk. Purposely."

"You weren't impolite," she demurred, her fore-head clearing. "Just...aloof."

"Right. I was going to make damn sure you stayed Allison's little friend and that's all." There, he'd said it. All of it. He itched to push her back against the sofa pillows, but he restrained himself so she had time to absorb what he'd just sprung on her.

Liz thought back to the times she'd sporadically seen Quentin during high school and college. "Once we got into that kind of relationship, it was hard to break out of it," she mused. "I got used to making polite chitchat with you."

"Yeah, once we fell into a pattern, it was hard to break it. Anyway, I figured you didn't like me too much anyway. I was distant and cool to you from the beginning."

She felt giddy. He'd desired her. He'd had to push her away. A wonderful shiver ran through her at the same time that she became aware of the intense look on his face and recognized the leashed desire there.

She let him take the coffee cup from her suddenly nervous fingers and deliberately place it on the coffee table next to his own. He picked up her hand then and kissed her wrist, her palm, his eyes never leaving hers. "I want you," he said, his voice smoky.

He searched her face and seemingly satisfied with the expression that he read there, he cupped the back of her neck and inexorably drew her toward him.

Her eyes drifted closed as his lips whispered over her eyes, her nose, her cheeks before, finally, settling on hers.

Liz melted into the kiss. His lips were smooth,

warm, enticing, and she nearly moaned in protest when they finally left hers to trail across her jaw, then down along the side of her neck. "Elizabeth," he said huskily.

She thrilled to the word, recognizing it now as a verbal caress. Would she ever be able to hear it again without being reminded of hot looks and smoldering desire?

"I hope to God we're not interrupted this time," he breathed against her neck, then pulled back to look at her. "Are you sure? Because I won't want to stop."

Any twinges of doubt she had were drowned in the overpowering desire coursing through her. "Yes. I'm sure," she heard herself say.

He must have heard the aching need in her voice, because he eased her back onto the pillows of the couch, careful to straighten her bad leg, and tugged on the zipper at the back of her dress until it rasped downward.

It seemed that she'd been waiting half a lifetime for this moment and in a way it was true. She'd felt an immediate physical attraction the first time she'd met him at eighteen.

His mouth latched onto a nipple through the thin, semi-transparent material of her bra and she gasped. He began a firm and rhythmic sucking that steadily increased the tension coiling within her.

She pulled at his T-shirt until she freed it from his waistband. "Help me," she pleaded.

He quickly sat up and his eyes burned into hers. He removed her bra and tossed it aside, then yanked his T-shirt over his head. When she moved to touch the well-sculpted muscles, thrown into relief by the lamplight, his hands closed on her wrists. "No," he said thickly, urgently, "need a bed. Now." Then he scooped her up and strode with her out of the room, up the stairs, and to his bedroom.

It was heavenly being carried by him, yet she tested his control by trailing her hands and lips over those parts of him that she could reach. He had a wonderful, corded neck, she decided. Strong and powerful and yet infinitely inviting to nibble on, especially near the pulse she found beating strong and quick. When she briefly lifted her head and noticed the tick working in his clenched jaw, she grew bolder, drawing his head down to hers.

"Holy Mary," he ground out, as he managed to get to the side of the bed and deposit her carefully on it.

Her dress was bunched at her waist. One sandal dangled precariously from her foot, the other having been lost somewhere on the way up the stairs. She kicked off the remaining shoe while he pulled off her dress and underpants.

He paused for a moment and grinned. "Red silk panties from Frederick's of Hollywood." He arched a brow. "You definitely have a thing for underwear," he murmured.

"They do mail order," she said unnecessarily, then added, "Muriel stopped by my house for some more of my things. She seems to have picked out my raciest underwear. There wasn't a plain cotton pair among them."

Quentin laughed huskily. "Remind me to give her a raise. Although," he paused, "it was unholy for her to bring back that stuff and then help deny me the pleasure of it for so long.''

He threw her clothes onto the nearby night table, and then she watched him divest himself of the remainder of his clothes. He was aroused, and when he came down beside her, she breathed in his musky male scent.

''You on top,'' he said. ''We don't want to hurt your ankle.'' Before she could protest, he'd carefully rolled her on top of him.

His hands intertwined with hers and he raised her arms above her head, leaving her vulnerable and exposed to his mouth, which took and plundered hers.

Liz felt the world shrink till nothing existed but the two of them and this moment. Her tongue dueled with his, her breasts pressed against his chest, his hair teasing her already sensitized nipples.

He gave a low groan, his erection hard against her, as his lips slid to her throat. ''That's right, yes,'' he whispered roughly. His hands pulled her even more firmly against him.

Her legs opened, slid around him, until he was there pushing up against the most secret aroused part of her. She'd wanted this for so long. Wanted him. One downward movement of her hips now and he'd be inside her, filling her in ways she'd only dreamed of.

''Quentin....'' She turned her head and met his hooded, smoky gaze.

''Say it,'' he muttered.

For a moment, she didn't understand. Then her heart leapt.

''Say you want me.''

Even as her heart cried out, she gave him the words he asked for. "I want you," she gasped and moved her hips, taking him in, feeling him stretch her, fill her. *I love you.*

Then he began to move inside her and her hips moved in counterpoint to his thrusts, undulating in a rhythm that matched the pace he set.

"That's it, honey. Yes," he coaxed. "Reach for it, baby."

She clenched around him spasmodically. "Quentin!!! Oh, please. Oh—yes!" Waves of sensation mixed with feeling and emotion wracked her.

He quickened his pace then, thrusting hard and fast. Her climax seemed to trigger his own. He threw back his head, gave a hoarse shout and surged into her one last time.

"Damn, sweetheart, you nearly killed me there." Quentin propped himself up on an elbow and caressed her thigh with his other hand. A thin sheen of sweat glistened on his skin.

It had been the most intense and satisfying sexual experience of his life. All he could think was: they should have done that a long time ago.

Liz hugged the sheet to her and waited for her racing heart to slow its pace. All she could think was: they should never have done that.

How could she ever have thought that going to bed with Quentin wouldn't cause a seismic shift in her world? And, oh God, they'd been so carried away, they hadn't even used protection! Although it was unlikely, there was a possibility that she might even now become pregnant.

The last thing she needed was for him to know just

how much she was affected, however, so she tried for sophisticated nonchalance. "You do know how to move fast," she said with a laugh that sounded forced to her own ears.

He chuckled. "You call eleven years of suppressed desire 'fast'?"

"Well, we're officially only on our—" she thought for a second "—second date. Although," she conceded, "things have been complicated by the fact that I've been living in your house."

He smiled wolfishly. "Yeah, that means you owe me at least two more dates." He paused. "By the terms of our agreement," he reminded her.

Liz quaked inwardly. Two more? Heaven help her, how was she going to survive two more dates with Quentin? He wanted a nice, uncomplicated business arrangement. And she…in the midst of their passion, she'd admitted to herself that she loved him.

There it was. She forced herself to examine the admission unflinchingly. What was she going to do?

He gave a quizzical half smile. "I'm different from the other men you've been with."

Yes, you're the only one I've been in love with. Yet, she could hardly answer with the truth.

She had, in fact, slept with only one other man. Soon after she'd learned of Quentin's engagement, she'd told herself to stop being silly and deluded. At twenty-three, it was time to give up hope Quentin would miraculously discover one day soon that he couldn't live without her.

So she'd finally accepted a date with Kevin Delaney, a nice, somewhat staid accountant who'd been hounding her for a date for at least six months. That Kevin's coloring and height gave him a more than passing resemblance to Quentin, she hadn't wanted to examine too closely.

Fireworks hadn't gone off, the world hadn't tilted on its axis, and she'd been forced to admit she'd made a terrible mistake.

There'd been men since then, of course, but nothing had gone beyond a few dates. The men had all been safe choices—as Allison uncannily liked to point out—unlikely to press her for more, content to let her set the pace.

Quentin broke into her thoughts with a teasing, "Am I supposed to take silence as an admission that I'm that good?"

If only he knew the truth! "Yes, well, everybody's unique," she managed in a strained voice.

Quentin frowned. He didn't like thinking about Elizabeth with other men. "Speaking from your wealth of experience?"

She was hugging the sheet to her if it were a life-line, unaware that the effect was to outline her ample chest—a chest he was intimately acquainted with now. "No, just one or two experiences."

One or two experiences? She'd gone to bed with him like a fall leaf hitting the ground at the first breeze. He couldn't resist asking, "So I compare favorably?"

"Yes." He had to bend his head to catch her monosyllabic response.

Troubled green eyes looked up into his. "I don't think this is going to work."

He tensed and stilled the hand caressing her thigh. "Meaning?"

She bit her lip and glanced away from him. "This is more complicated than I thought it would be."

He experienced an emotion suspiciously akin to panic at the thought that she might be trying to back out of their plan. Yet a part of him acknowledged that she was right. Going to bed with her had rocked his world.

Aloud he tried, "There's nothing complicated about two people who are attracted to each other acting on that attraction. I'd say this is as simple as it gets." His voice sounded hard to his own ears.

She turned back to him. "You know, it's more than that. We're talking about having a baby. Bringing a baby into this world through a business arrangement, instead of because two people love each other enough to get married and have a baby together."

He frowned. "You make it sound like most marriages are flawless relationships. The fact is they're usually far from that." Panic made him perversely willing to argue with her instead of pushing her back against the pillows and using more primitive ways to persuade her.

"How can you be so cynical when your parents have a marriage that anyone would envy?" she asked with a troubled look on her face.

He sighed. After the debacle with Vanessa, he himself had pondered what made his parents' relationship work. "My parents are the exception. They didn't see each other for two years when Dad was in the military. They almost eloped because my grandparents objected to my mother getting married before she finished college. They had lots of time to paint rosy pictures of each other, and, believe me, even then, their marriage hasn't been a walk in the park. Dad was so busy building his company that my mother basically raised us on her own."

Liz sat up in bed, careful to keep the sheet from falling and exposing her breasts. "The exception is what I've been looking for." She twisted the sheet nervously in her fists. "What I'm willing to wait for."

Quentin's face was devoid of expression, giving her no clue as to what he was thinking. "This was a m-mistake." She took a deep breath to steady her voice. "I'm sorry."

"You want out of our agreement," he said flatly, his hooded gaze revealing nothing.

"Y-yes," she whispered.

He sat up and swung himself out of bed. Her gaze raked down his muscled back, tight buttocks, and strong legs. She drank in the sight before he started to dress.

When he turned back to her, he wore a cool and remote expression. "This was what we agreed on, nothing more and nothing less," he said smoothly. "One of us could have stopped the whole thing at any time during our four dates."

She willed herself not to cry. She bit her lip and looked away. "Well, I wouldn't worry about anything. With my condition, it will be difficult to get pregnant even at the right time—which this isn't."

Nine

Thirty-eight, thirty-nine, forty. She finished counting the days on the calendar in her hand.

She was late. No question. How was that possible? With her condition, getting pregnant should have been difficult. Yet one night, one unforgettable night, in Quentin's arms, had been enough.

Panic assaulted her. She'd have to visit her doctor to confirm. But she already knew the diagnosis. She was never this late.

She'd done a good job of avoiding Quentin since that fateful night. He'd reluctantly agreed to drive her home after she'd agreed to allow Muriel to come over and help her for the next few days—until she could walk without the crutches.

In fact, since that night she hadn't seen Quentin and had dealt only with Noah about the day-care project.

If Noah had thought it strange that she and Quentin didn't deal directly with each other, he kept his thoughts to himself.

She'd been miserable, of course. She'd lost weight in the past month, which made the pregnancy a double surprise. She'd have to force herself to eat more now for the sake of the baby.

If only she could deal with her problem sleeping through the night as easily. Since leaving Quentin's house, she'd lain awake many a night thinking about what to do.

Yet, she hadn't been able to work up any interest in the literature she'd collected at the sperm bank.

She thought back to the night she'd lain in Quentin's arms. Their mutual desire, once unleashed, had been a force greater than either of them, demanding satisfaction. Afterward, she'd become frightened by the emotions he'd aroused in her and what she'd allowed herself to admit in a moment of passion: she loved him.

She'd reacted by retreating, doubting whether she could go on with their plan without incredible heartache. And Quentin had exited her life, a tacit understanding between them that they'd both "forget" their night of shared passion and go on with their lives.

The trouble was, in less than nine months, they'd have a very real and constant reminder of that night!

Liz's visit to the doctor's office the next Friday confirmed what she already knew. If the doctor was surprised at the rapid turn of events, he didn't show it.

After receiving instructions from the doctor about appropriate supplements, collecting what seemed like three dozen pamphlets on childbirth, and scheduling her next visit, she left the doctor's office and drove home.

What was she going to do? She might be able to convince everyone she'd been artificially inseminated in such a short time, but what would she do when the baby arrived? What if it was a little boy with the Whittaker trademark gray eyes? How long before her secret would become known?

Of course, she could move to another town. Maybe even join her father down in Florida. But that would mean folding up Precious Bundles and starting again from scratch.

No, she had to face reality, which was bearing Quentin's child right here in Carlyle, which was Whittaker family home turf.

Sooner or later she'd have to tell Quentin, of course. But, please God, not now.

She needed time to marshal her forces. Time to think. And, Lord knew she didn't want Quentin to think she was going to him for money. That would only confirm his opinion of women and their motives.

Ordinarily, she'd turn to Allison in moments like these. Ally was at her best in crises. But she knew what Allison's reaction would be. She'd be overjoyed that the plot she'd originally set in motion had come to fruition. She'd insist on telling Quentin right away and having him assume his responsibilities—financial or otherwise—or else.

Arriving home, she dropped her purse on a side

table and headed toward her desk. The only other person she could trust was her father. And he wouldn't be happy.

She chewed on her lower lip and eyed the phone on the desk as if it had been possessed by evil spirits.

How her father would react to the news that his only child—his unmarried daughter—was pregnant, heaven only knew.

Well, best to get the inevitable over with, she decided. Grimly, she picked up the receiver and dialed her father's number. His greeting a second later made her stomach twist in knots.

Patrick Donovan immediately started in on his favorite topic: his only child's recalcitrance about calling and visiting. "Lizzie, if you're too busy to come down here, I'll come to you instead. It'll do me some good to see the lads."

By lads, of course, her Dad meant his sixty-ish buddies, business associates, and fishing companions, many of whom had yet to be lured to sunny Florida, despite, she was sure, Patrick Donovan's formidable sales pitch.

Her father having given her an opening, she took a deep breath and plunged in. "I'm glad you're planning to come up here. How about Labor Day Weekend, Christmas, and, let's say, the middle of next April?"

Her father laughed. "Ah, it warms my heart, it does, that you're so anxious to see me. And what would next April be, if you don't mind my askin'?"

She closed her eyes. "Having a baby. No due date

yet. But if we're lucky, you'll be here for the blessed event.''

There was a pause at the other end.

"Dad?" she asked uncertainly, opening her eyes.

"What!" She heard him mutter under his breath. "When I said I was lookin' forward to the pitter-patter of li'l feet, sweet pea, I thought it was clear I preferred for you to be married at the time. Seems like I was right to worry about you up there all alone.''

She winced. She'd known he would be disappointed in her. Still, it didn't make things any easier to hear him give voice to it.

"Next you'll be tellin' me who the father is, no doubt," her father grumbled.

She steeled herself for what was to come. "Quentin Whittaker.''

"Saints alive!" Then, "Whittaker, is it?"

"Now, Dad, don't be angry—"

"Angry?" Her father gave a hearty laugh. "I'm de-light-ed!''

"What?" He couldn't have shocked her more if he'd just announced plans to give up fishing and join an order of Franciscan monks.

Her father chuckled. "Well, I'm going to be a granddaddy. Now, mind you, that's enough to warm my heart. But, sweet pea, you've also managed to bring the family business back into the family!''

"What are you talking about?" For a moment, she wondered about the onset of senility, then dismissed the thought. Her father was as sharp as a tack.

"Quentin owns most of what was Donovan Construction, Lizzie.''

"Wha—? How?" Her world tilted on its axis. It wasn't possible!

"Oh, he didn't buy it outright," her father continued chattily. "No, he bought it from Scudder Brothers about a year after I sold out to them. Quentin is the major shareholder in a holding company called Samtech Enterprises that now owns what used to be Donovan Construction."

Liz's head began to pound. The enormity of her predicament hit her like a ton of bricks. It was even worse than she'd realized...for she'd unwittingly played into her father's hands.

Her father thought she'd just provided him with the keys to a business it had taken him a lifetime to build. A company she'd always wondered if he would have sold if he'd had a son to enter the still testosterone-dominated construction business. Now, with any luck and with Quentin's help, he had the chance to pass the business along to a grandson.

Her father suddenly asked suspiciously, "He asked you to marry him, hasn't he, sweet pea?"

Liz felt her temper begin to rise. Why, her father already had her at the altar! "I haven't told him."

"You have'n— In the name of all the saints, why not?" her father boomed. "At least have him own up to his responsibility."

A responsibility, was she? "Maybe I don't want to marry him, have you thought about that?" Let him chew on that for a while! "I'll tell him about the baby in my own time," she warned, "and don't even try to interfere!"

"Now don't get your back up, sweet pea—"

"Don't sweet pea me. I don't need another man trying to tell me what to do!" She sounded shrill but she was beyond caring.

Her father's rumbling laugh sounded over the phone. "Tried to tell you what to do, did he? He'll learn. Donovan temper's one to be reckoned with."

"Goodbye, Dad." She dropped the receiver back in its cradle.

How could Quentin own Donovan Construction and she not know it? Because he didn't own it directly...and because he hadn't mentioned it to her!

Suddenly she had a more ominous thought. What if Quentin had purposely kept the information from her? She thought back to the Fourth of July concert and their conversation about her father. Surely he must have known then, if not before, that she would have considered that tidbit of information very important.

While she'd been spilling her most private thoughts and fears about proving herself to her father, he'd known—known!—that he held Donovan Construction! When had he planned to share that information with her, she wondered?

She drummed her fingers on the desk and narrowed her eyes. Maybe in the delivery room? Yes, she could see it now. Quentin and her father having a nice little chuckle over her prone and exhausted body, which had just brought forth the much anticipated little Whittaker-Donovan heir.

She could just throttle Quentin! After what she'd told him, he must have known she would be unwittingly playing into her father's hands. And, yet, he hadn't warned her. Hadn't said anything at all but had made mad, passionate love to her.

Hurt intruded where the anger was. She'd trusted him! Shared feelings with him that she'd never voiced to anyone else.

Well, she'd show him. She wasn't some little thing that needed to be protected from the truth, manipulated, or told what to do. She'd have her baby on her own and she'd manage just fine!

"She's what?"

"Liz is pregnant."

Quentin stared at his sister. All his life she'd been the bearer of news designed to bring upheaval to his life, but she'd just surpassed herself, whether she knew it or not.

Elizabeth pregnant. He was going to be a father. "How pregnant is she?"

Allison's lips quirked and she quipped, "Oh, you know, just a little bit."

Quentin prayed for patience. "How far along is she?" He already knew, but he wanted the confirmation his instincts were right.

Allison gave him a quizzical look. "I don't know. She didn't say."

"Did she tell you who the father is?" Quentin demanded.

"She went to a fertility clinic—"

Quentin's hands bunched into fists. Was that possible? Had Elizabeth followed through on her plans for artificial insemination soon after their night together? Was this baby not a Whittaker after all? His jaw tightened. There was one way to find out.

He strode out of his office and Allison hurried after him. "Quentin, where are you—"

"I'll be out this afternoon," he informed his secretary as he aimed for the elevators beyond the reception area. "I'm not reachable."

"You're always reachable," Allison piped up as she tried to keep pace with him. "Where are you headed?"

Quentin ignored the question. The elevator arrived and he stepped in, turning to face Allison, who was insisting on answers.

"Just what's happened between you and Liz?"

"I'll let you know as soon as I find out," he told her before the doors closed.

His mind worked furiously as he drove to Elizabeth's house, keeping just the wrong side of the speed limit. What if the baby was his? Had she been planning to keep it from him? Or had she really gone from his arms to the cold and clinical ones of a fertility doctor? He felt a nerve begin to twitch at his temple.

One thing was for sure. If this baby was a Whittaker, he was going to make damn sure Elizabeth acknowledged the kid's paternity.

He pulled up in front of Precious Bundles, and strode to the door, taking the porch steps two at a time. An OPEN sign showed through the paneled glass. As he let himself in, he turned to give it a flick.

Elizabeth sat at her antique desk, cradling the phone between her shoulder and one ear and jotting notes on a pad in front of her. Her eyes widened the minute he entered. "Y-y-yes, Mrs. Bradford, the wallpaper should be delivered Tuesday."

He walked to the desk and leaned over, planting his hands on the smooth mahogany finish. She scribbled something and the pencil point broke from the pressure.

As she reached for something else to write with from the pencil holder, he caught hold of her hand, forcing her to look up. Get off the phone, he mouthed and then let go of her hand.

"O-o-okay," she stammered and he was unsure who she was addressing. Maybe it was for both his benefit and Mrs. Bradford's. "Yes, right. Speak with you on Tuesday."

Liz set the phone in its cradle and looked up at Quentin. He looked like a tiger ready to pounce.

"One question." His voice was deceptively soft. "Is it mine?"

His slate-gray eyes caught and held hers. Magnetic, intense, relentless in their scrutiny.

"Yes."

His shoulders relaxed and a little bit of tension seemed to roll out of him. "You told Allison that you'd used a sperm donor," he accused.

"No, she just assumed and I let her think that. Anyway, it's not a lie. You were one of the first donors she suggested."

"When were you going to tell me?" he demanded.

That did it. Anger was the last thing she was willing to take from him! "About the time you decided to tell me that you own my father's company!" She rose from her seat. He still towered over her, of course, but at least she no longer felt like a criminal being interrogated under a strobe light.

She unflinchingly met his stormy gray eyes until he turned away and began to pace in front of her desk. "I didn't think it was important. At first, I wasn't even sure if you knew or not."

"After the Boston Pops concert, you knew it would matter to me but you said nothing!"

He stopped to face her again. "All right, I should have told you. But right now, we have a bigger problem. You're pregnant and we need to figure out what to do."

His cavalier dismissal of her concerns about Donovan Construction fueled her temper. "We? I thought we agreed there would be no 'we.'"

He smiled grimly. "That was before I knew I was going to be a father."

"Well, don't worry then. You're not," she snapped.

"I fathered the child you're carrying!" His eyes narrowed. "Or were you lying?"

"I admit you made a small contribution. That's a far cry from saying you're going to be a father."

"A small contribution?" he snarled as he advanced. "I'd say it was a major contribution to our mutual enjoyment."

"I was raised by a single parent, and the baby and I will be just fine on our own."

He halted, seemingly arrested by her words, and then stuffed his hands in his pockets. "So you know that a single parent can do just fine, but having two helps."

She'd made him furious, and surprisingly she didn't get nearly as much satisfaction from that as she thought she would.

A muscle twitched in his jaw. "Your baby is a Whittaker. Are you sure you want to deny your child all the advantages that entails?"

She met his gaze steadily. "I wouldn't deny you access to the baby, if that's what you really want. But," she added, "despite whatever you may believe about women, money isn't what I want. For myself or this baby."

He frowned and seemed to choose his words carefully. "All things considered, whatever I believe about your motives isn't relevant anymore."

"It's very relevant." She shook her head. "Listen to yourself! You're talking about all the material things you could provide for this baby."

He looked grim. "That's the customary male role. Breadwinner. Provider. Are you going to deny me that?"

"I'm not going to deny you anything important, Quentin. I'm not going to stop you from seeing your son or daughter. But I don't need anything else." Except you, always you.

He looked like he was about to say something and then changed his mind. He nodded curtly, turned on his heel and stalked out.

Liz sagged into her chair and finally allowed herself to give in to the tears. She'd accomplished what she'd set out to do, which was tell him off and take a stand about being able to raise the baby on her own. So why did she feel so miserable?

* * *

That night Allison dropped by unannounced. In her typical no-nonsense style, her friend wasted no time in cutting to the chase. "Lizzie, when I mentioned you were pregnant, Quentin left his office like he had the devil nipping at his heels."

"Allison, I—" Liz swallowed. It was going to be hard to broach this subject with her friend, no matter how long they'd known each other, no matter how many secrets they'd shared. They were in her living room, Allison having just dropped into an armchair while Liz took the couch.

"Have you talked to him?" Allison demanded. "I swear, if he's insulted you, I'll, I'll—" Allison paused for breath. "Well, I don't know what I'll do exactly, but it will be really painful for him."

"Ally—"

"He can be overprotective, but that doesn't mean he needs to pull his boorish older brother routine with you." Allison fumed. "I mean, he already has me for that! And besides, he has to respect you for deciding—"

"Ally, I'm having Quentin's baby."

"What?" For once Allison looked flummoxed. "How…? Why…?"

"You missed 'where' and 'when,'" Liz said dryly.

"Now's not the time to joke around!" Allison's brows knitted. She tossed the cushion she'd been toying with on the coffee table and walked over the fireplace.

Liz had known this was going to be difficult. She just hoped Allison wouldn't be mad at her forever.

Right now, Allison looked a lot like her courtroom self.

"Okay, I think I just ran through several emotions there." Allison blew a breath. "You're in luck because angry and hurt passed in about two seconds, and now I'm just happy."

"Oh, Ally." She should have known Allison would be loyal.

"How could you not have spilled the beans?" Ally held her hands out in exasperation. "You let me think...well, you know."

Liz cleared her throat. She and Ally had had very few secrets from each other, but this one was a doozy. "You're Quentin's sister. You would have felt compelled to tell him about the baby, and knowing you, you would have browbeat him, too." She gave a weak smile, then added, "Anyway, we had a terrible argument."

Allison's eyes widened. "Ooh, I would have loved to see that! Quentin never gets out of control. Ruins the cool CEO persona."

"I provoked him," she admitted.

Allison chuckled and folded her arms across her chest. "Even better. Was he furious that you hadn't told him right away about the baby?"

"Not only that. *I was angry.* Did you know that Quentin owns Donovan Construction through a holding company?"

Allison's mouth dropped open, then she strode over to plop herself back down in the armchair, seeming to need the support. "Oh, my."

"Oh, yes. A crucial fact he failed to mention even after he…we…." She felt her face heat.

"I see."

"My father's ecstatic. I'm not only going to produce the long-awaited grandbaby, but I'll be bringing the family business back into the family. Quentin will carefully manage it, of course, until—" she crossed her fingers and let her voice drip with sarcasm "—with any luck, it passes to the wee grandson."

"Agh."

She nodded grimly. "Exactly."

"What was Quentin's reaction?"

If only he'd had one! "He figures he should have told me about the company, but he didn't think it was important enough to mention at first."

Allison rolled her eyes.

"He insists on accepting financial responsibility for the baby."

"Naturally. Quentin's been accepting responsibility since he was in the cradle."

Liz nodded. It was part of why she loved him. But she couldn't—wouldn't—let him act out of responsibility here. "Right. Well, I won't let him do it."

"What?" Allison looked alarmed, then leaned forward in the armchair. "What do you mean?"

"I mean," Liz said firmly, "we made a mistake. Since I was the one who wanted to get pregnant, I'm prepared to raise the baby on my own."

"Mistake? Are you nuts?" Allison jumped up and planted her hands on her hips. "Do you think my brother goes around impregnating women like that?" Allison snapped her fingers, then shook her head. "Of course not. Quentin never does anything impetuous. He wants you. Otherwise you'd never be having his baby.''

Of course Allison wanted everything to be wrapped up tidily. After all, she was the one who early on had come up with the scheme of using Quentin as a sperm donor. Liz sighed inwardly. ''Want is different from love.''

''No, want is the road to love.''

''He doesn't even like me.''

Allison quirked a brow in a way that reminded Liz of Quentin. ''Oh, come now.'' She folded her hands behind her back and started to pace. ''Let's examine the evidence, shall we? My brother has avoided entanglements for the last seven years. Within weeks of meeting you again and hiring you for the day care, he breaks one of his own golden rules by mixing business with pleasure.''

Allison stopped and threw her a piercing look. ''Not only that, but he does this knowing he's playing with fire. After all, you're a woman who's desperate to have a baby. Inexplicably though, he gets angry when you talk about artificial insemination and tells you to get a husband instead!'' Allison rested her hands on the back of the armchair and leaned over it. ''Then he all but volunteers for the job himself!''

Liz nearly smiled. Allison making a case was a sight to behold, even when it was at her expense. And although Allison couldn't have known about Quentin's idea that they consider a marriage of convenience to have a baby, she'd come remarkably close to the truth.

"I'm dying of curiosity, but I'm not going to ask exactly how this happened—'' Allison paused and gave her a knowing look ''—though I'd make a good listener if anybody needed one. Let's just say I know one thing and that is that you and Quentin have more chemistry than I've seen since high school.''

Liz sighed.

"You love him, don't you?''

The unexpected question and Allison's understanding look caused unexpected tears to well in Liz's eyes.

Darn. She didn't want to cry in front of Allison, but there was little she could do to hide the wetness of her eyes.

"Oh, Lizzie!'' Allison sat down next to her, and gave her a quick hug. ''It's okay.''

"N-n-no, it's not,'' Liz choked out. ''I've made a complete mess of things.''

Allison frowned. ''You? I'd say Quentin's at least equally responsible if you want to call this a mess.''

Liz stifled a sob. ''All I wanted to do was have a baby.''

"And you are! And I'm going to be an aunt!'' Allison laughed. ''And my mother—oh my gosh, Mom is going to be ecstatic!''

"About my trapping her son?'' she warbled.

"No, silly, about you and a grandbaby! This has been near the top of her wish list for a while.''

"What do you mean?'' Liz looked at her friend's suddenly sheepish face.

"Well, er—''

Realization dawned. ''I've been an open book, haven't I?'' She'd gone out of her way for years not to show any particular interest when Quentin's name was mentioned. She could have saved herself the effort, it seemed.

Allison grinned. "It was hard to miss your hero worship."

"I'd gotten over that," Liz protested. At the very least, she liked to think her teenage crush had developed into more mature feelings.

Allison rolled her eyes. "Thank goodness. Quentin's my brother, and I think he's pretty terrific, but the stuff of fairy tales he's not."

Liz gave a choked laugh.

"See, you agree with me!" Allison gave her a quick, reassuring squeeze, then said briskly, "So, don't even try to give me any nonsense about Quentin. He deserves to get all the diaper-changing misery one man can get. And as for you and him, everything will work out, you'll see."

Ten

Liz felt under siege. Her father was threatening to come up from Florida and "set things to rights." As Allison had predicted, Quentin's mother was over the moon about the baby, and had called to say that if there was anything Liz needed, she and James would be there before Liz finished asking.

In her typical tactful way, Ava had acted as if there was nothing in the least bit shocking about her thirty-six-year-old unmarried eldest son having suddenly impregnated her daughter's long-standing best friend.

But if Liz thought Quentin had inherited his mother's tact, she was wrong. Dead wrong.

One minute she was speaking with the construction contractor for the day care, the next she felt the hair on the nape of her neck rise and stir.

"I want to talk to you."

She eyed him warily. He was looking every inch the corporate executive today, a black, custom-tailored suit set off with a power-yellow tie. "I'm speaking with Mr. Higgins."

He ignored the frigidity in her voice and took her arm. "I'm sure this can wait while I discuss some urgent business with you." She found herself led away as the contractor readily took the hint and went back to his work.

The minute they were alone in the hall, she turned on him, incensed. "That was rude."

He shrugged. "He works for me. Don't worry about it."

"Oh, is that the way of it?" she answered in an icy voice fit to do Patrick Donovan proud. "People are just supposed to defer to your desires? No one would dare defy the mighty Quentin Whittaker, hmm?"

He ran a hand through his hair in a gesture she was coming to recognize as a sign of his frustration. "Have you been thinking about how you're going to manage with this baby? And keep Precious Bundles afloat?"

So that's why he was here. "I'll manage. I will not accept money from you," she responded firmly and, she hoped, repressively.

"You're already accepting money from me, remember? The day-care project for Whittaker Enterprises," he said coolly.

Uneasiness stirred in her stomach. "That's different."

"Is it? What would happen if I decided the day care was something the company no longer needed?"

Her eyes widened at the implied threat. "That would be breach of contract—"

"Even if you could afford to sue, which we both know you can't," he continued, his voice holding a touch of steel, "I could afford a settlement. But it might take a while to negotiate."

He didn't need to add what they both knew. She couldn't afford to wait for a settlement. Suddenly she understood why Quentin had the business reputation he had—he had earned it. And now she was the target of his ruthless business methods.

But something about the set, closed look he wore made her check her temper and, instead, study him, tensed for her answer.

He'd been hurt in the past, she knew, and he was clearly going to protect himself from being that vulnerable to a woman again. That had obviously led him to the conclusion that he ought to bargain with her as he would deal with a business rival. Just as he'd originally tried to strike a deal with her for a baby and a marriage of convenience. A deal that had gone hopelessly awry and landed them...here.

Armed with that realization, she found herself asking, "What are you suggesting?"

"Marry me."

Her heart leapt, but she forced her voice to remain level. "Why?"

"You're having my baby, that's why."

"That doesn't mean you have to marry me."

He frowned. "In my book it does." He regarded her intently. "I've thought about this from all the angles, and this is the best solution. We'll get married—at least until after the baby is born.''

When she started to protest, he held up his hand. ''Hear me out. It's best for you, me, and the baby. We'll go through with the original plan but this time we'll do it for the short haul. I want the baby to be born a Whittaker. And my parents will get the grandchild they've been pining for, and which they think it's my duty to produce *legitimately*.''

She couldn't resist asking, ''What do I get?''

He paused for a second, as if the question had caught him off guard. ''You get peace of mind. Financial support to make sure the baby is always well cared for. Financial support to make sure Precious Bundles stays afloat until you can focus on it again.''

Liz repressed a twinge of hurt. She'd known he was treating this like a financial bargain. What had she expected? she silently scolded herself. A declaration of undying love?

Aloud, she said coolly, ''I'll think about it.''

When he didn't respond—didn't even move a muscle, actually—she started feeling uncomfortable. ''Have you finished?''

His eyes narrowed. ''No, dammit! I haven't.'' Before she could register what he was about, he grabbed her arms and his mouth came down on hers in a hard kiss. He made sure she felt all of his frustration before setting her roughly back away from him.

''Let me know when you've thought about it,'' he bit out before turning and striding away.

* * *

I'll think about it?

Quentin thought he'd never dealt with a more contrary female in his life. And that was saying something, considering who he was related to!

He ached just looking at her, wanting to strip her naked and make love to her thoroughly, and all she could do was look at him with those amazing green-gold eyes and say coolly, *I'll think about it?*

Okay, yeah, maybe he should have told her about owning Donovan Construction. At first he hadn't thought it was important and then he'd delayed telling her until it was too late.

He gazed out of the windows of his office, his hands shoved deep into his trouser pockets. He could see the office towers across the highway, part of the hi-tech corridor outside Carlyle, and, more distantly, the green of verdant hills. He often liked to chew on a problem this way, contemplating the distant Massachusetts landscape.

He'd bungled the plan, of course. He'd meant to approach Elizabeth with infallible logic. Persuade her that getting married was the best option.

But instead of making her see how much she needed him to keep Precious Bundles going while she had their baby, he'd used—he winced as his mind flirted with the dirty word—blackmail.

Once she'd started again on not needing his money, his response had been driven by pure male need for dominance and control.

Except was that really it? No, it was his need for her, he realized, that had made him lose his head. Her and the baby, of course. For he realized, he wanted this baby—his baby and Elizabeth's—with an intensity that surprised him.

If only the darn woman would cooperate with his plan to set things right.

To add insult to injury, his whole family seemed to have taken sides and they weren't flying the Whittaker colors.

His thoughts drifted back to that morning when his sister had stalked into his office unannounced. She'd been angry and had let him have a piece of her mind. It was her parting shot that had stayed with him all day however.

Allison had jabbed a finger into his chest and had accused, "You tried to bully her into accepting your terms! You threw money at her because you think she's just like Vanessa and that's all she's interested in. Isn't that right?"

"Are you nuts?" he'd growled back, still sensitive about his admittedly deplorable behavior and quasi-blackmail of Elizabeth. "I wouldn't use their names in the same sentence."

"Why should I believe you?"

When he failed to respond, Allison had stalked out, leaving him to chew over her question.

He gazed at the landscape in front of him now. And thought about Allison's question again.

Why?

Because it was ridiculous, that's why. Vanessa represented everything he abhorred. She was greedy and manipulative. And she'd taught him a tough lesson in life and love.

He paused and puzzled over that.

Love? Had he really loved Vanessa?

The feelings he'd had for her paled in comparison to those he felt for Elizabeth. In fact, he'd spent the past three days in purgatory waiting for Elizabeth to decide either to open the gates of paradise to him or...well, the alternative didn't bear contemplating.

So why did he persist in believing Vanessa had betrayed his love, while believing he didn't love Elizabeth?

Realization dawned like the sun spreading its rays across a new morning sky.

He was afraid of the power Elizabeth would have over him if he admitted anything he felt for her came close to being spelled l-o-v-e. If Vanessa had hurt him, Elizabeth's ability to wound him would be enough to send him to his knees.

But dammit. He did love Elizabeth. And it was because she was the antithesis of Vanessa. She was caring, sweet, vulnerable.

His family thought he was the bad guy, but the truth was, he hadn't been able to put Elizabeth out of his mind. His thoughts had an alarming tendency to drift off during conference calls at work, meetings with clients—in fact, just about anywhere.

He supposed he had no choice now but to wait for her response to his proposal. It was her move.

He could think of only one way to tip the odds in his favor. One way to obliterate what he'd said and make it her decision to marry him and have the baby be born a Whittaker...unpressured by his ownership of Donovan Construction and by his money.

He reached for the phone and dialed his lawyer.

He'd just finished the call when a booming voice from the reception area caught his attention.

Just what he needed. Another unexpected visitor. He was still recovering from Allison's "visit" that morning. When he got to the reception area, however, he came to a dead halt.

It had been a few years, but he still recognized the burly Irishman.

Elizabeth's father. Great timing.

"Mr. Donovan." He made his tone respectful.

Patrick Donovan turned from Celine and raised bushy eyebrows. Although Quentin had the height advantage by a good two inches in his estimate, the older man was still able to look him in the eyes.

"Now, now, lad. We're practically family. I'll have none of that Mr. Donovan stuff. It's Patrick."

"Er—Patrick then."

Elizabeth's father nodded toward Celine, who'd risen from her desk chair. "I was just tellin' this beautiful lady that I was here to see you but I didn't have an appointment."

At the word "beautiful," Quentin watched in fascination as a shade of pink stained Celine's cheeks.

Well, well. Looked like his longtime secretary might have met her match in the charm department.

Quentin gestured behind him to his office. "You don't need an appointment," he said smoothly. "Come on in."

"Don't mind if I do."

"Celine, hold my calls."

She nodded. "Of course."

Patrick preceded him into his office and Quentin

walked to the minibar set up in an alcove. "It's early, but can I get you anything?" He felt like a scotch himself.

Patrick settled himself in a leather chair at right angles to the couch. "Scotch. On the rocks. It's early but not early enough."

Quentin poured scotch into two glasses and handed one to Patrick. "I'm going to guess that Elizabeth doesn't know you've come to see me."

"And you'd be right." They both downed some scotch. "Always knew you were a quick study."

Quentin leaned forward and rested his elbows on his knees, nursing his glass between two hands. "What did she tell you?" he asked, testing.

"Just that she'd finally broken the news about the baby to you."

So his marriage proposal hadn't reached Patrick's ears. He figured she wouldn't tell her father until her mind was made up. No use raising false hopes.

"Can't say I was happy to hear my daughter was pregnant out of wedlock."

Quentin nodded, wondering if Elizabeth had ever told her father about her medical condition. The answer appeared to be no, so he just kept silent. Heck, even her medical condition didn't explain why *he* was the one who'd impregnated her.

"What's done is done, however." A smile suddenly creased Patrick's face. "And a grandbaby is a grandbaby."

Quentin sipped the scotch. Well, at least he had Patrick's approval in one direction.

"Mind you, I won't see Liz hurt. But I've got a feeling that you two will work out your problems."

Quentin wished he were that optimistic. He cleared his throat. "Has she said anything to you about Donovan Construction?"

Patrick's brows snapped together. "Yes, breathing fire and brimstone last time I talked to her about it."

Quentin grimaced.

"'Course I was pleased as punch about that part at least." Patrick's brows lifted. "Bringing the company back into the family, so to speak." The older man leaned forward suddenly. "You would pass on Donovan Construction to the baby, wouldn't you?"

"It's part of the baby's heritage as far as I'm concerned. I wouldn't sell it." He paused. "Whether Elizabeth accepts my marriage proposal or not."

Patrick sat back, satisfied. "Glad we see eye to eye."

And Quentin was beginning to see even more. And to understand just why Elizabeth had been so angry about the whole Donovan Construction business. Her father obviously saw the company as an added little dividend to becoming a grandfather.

He cleared his throat. He had to tread carefully here. "She wants to be respected for her accomplishments, not for whom she married." If she agreed to marry him, that was, he added silently.

"'Course she wants to be respected for her accomplishments," Patrick said, calling him back from his thoughts. "Worked damned hard to start that business of hers." Patrick swirled the golden liquid in his glass.

Quentin thought about the question he wanted to

ask, then decided to go ahead and ask it. "Why did you sell Donovan Construction, if I can ask?"

Patrick sighed and settled back in the chair. "Construction's a tough business and it's gotten harder for the little guys to stay afloat. When I retired, selling seemed like the right move. The business had a better chance of surviving as part of a bigger company. Figured I was making the right decision for most of the employees, saving their jobs in the long haul."

"You never considered having Elizabeth run the company?"

Patrick's frowned. "Good God, no!" The fingers of one hand drummed on the arm of his chair. "Why in the world would she have wanted to get involved in a down-and-dirty business like construction? 'Sides, she was building a nice career for herself in architecture."

"Maybe because there was a little company with the name 'Donovan' stuck on it." Quentin took a sip of his scotch and regarded the older man steadily over the rim of the glass. He was treading on dangerous territory, but he knew he needed some answers if he was ever going to build a lasting relationship with Elizabeth.

Patrick was silent for a minute, digesting the information he'd been given. "Would have been a fool's errand, in any case. As I said, the company wasn't viable on its own in the long run. Not the way the construction business was going."

Quentin nodded in agreement. "Did you ever talk to Elizabeth about your motivation for selling?"

Patrick sighed. "No, I don't think I ever did. I

guess I should have.'' Gazing out the window, he added, ''Wouldn't have wanted her to get any silly notion that I was selling because I didn't trust her.''

Quentin gazed out the window, too, relieved that he'd gotten his point across. ''The thing is, Elizabeth does have a head for business, she's driven and she's got a vision of what she wants.''

''That she does,'' Patrick concurred, a note of pride in his voice.

''Why don't you tell her that sometime?'' Quentin met Patrick's eyes, green like Elizabeth's only without the golden touches. ''Even the best of us need to hear the words occasionally.''

Patrick paused a moment, considering, then nodded slowly. ''I will. That I will,'' he said gruffly.

Attempting to lighten the mood, Quentin chuckled and rubbed his chin. ''You think the world is ready for Donovan-Whittaker offspring?''

Patrick slapped him on the back, tacitly acknowledging the newfound understanding between them. ''I've wondered myself.''

Liz spent a sleepless night tossing and turning. As soon as she seemed to drift off, her dreams were of Quentin. Quentin asking her to marry him. Quentin making love to her. Quentin amused, irritated, annoyed.

She got out of bed at seven, and noted that her face showed her sleeplessness. She looked bleary-eyed, and worse.

She padded around in her robe and nightie, fixing herself eggs, toast and juice. God, she missed her morning cup of coffee. But she'd sworn off caffeine the minute she'd discovered she was pregnant.

Once she had a food-laden tray, she moved to the living room. She placed the tray on the coffee table and eased herself onto the couch to watch the morning news.

Quentin had not called. It had been three days. Isn't that what she wanted though? Still some small part of her, she guessed, had wanted him to continue pursuing her, refusing to take no for an answer.

At noon, the phone rang when she was going through some antique auction catalogs.

Her first thought was: Quentin! Then she felt irritated for the way her pulse raced. Even if it was him, she needed to remain calm and collected.

In fact, it wasn't Quentin, but his lawyer.

"Ms. Donovan," the attorney intoned, "I spoke with Mr. Whittaker this morning and he requested I call you regarding the terms of your, ah, financial agreement."

Her hand tightened on the receiver. "Yes."

"Mr. Whittaker has authorized me to transfer all of his shares in Samtech Industries to your name. Are you agreeable to such an arrangement, Ms. Donovan?"

Her world spun around and her hands felt clammy. "Yes," she managed, fighting to keep her composure. What had Quentin done?

"Good. I'll finalize all the paperwork for the transfer of shares and I'll contact you at the end of the week when the documents are ready to sign." The lawyer ended the call with a final word about information he'd need from her.

Liz replaced the receiver in a daze. Quentin had decided to hand Donovan Construction over to her. And in the process, she realized, he'd gotten rid of her fear that by accepting his marriage proposal she'd be playing into her father's hands.

But why?

Even for a man intent on taking financial responsibility for fathering a baby, it was a generous gesture.

Unless he didn't do it just for the baby, her heart whispered. There was no stipulation that she'd hold the company shares in trust for their child.

It almost sounded like one of those grand gestures only a man blinded by love would make. A man intent on proving to the woman he loved that he trusted her, that she had nothing to prove except to herself.

Could it be?

She realized how big a leap it was for him to trust a woman after having been treated so shabbily by Vanessa. She pressed shaky fingers to her lips.

He'd confessed to wanting her. Feeling an unwanted attraction from the time he'd first met her. She desperately wanted to believe....

Yet, if she loved him, wasn't he worth fighting for? He might not love her. But at least she was sure he wanted her, and if Allison was right, they were on to something that could become deeper and more lasting...with her help.

She looked at the clock and then picked up the phone. For her plan to work, she'd need Allison's help. This time, she had her own proposition to offer Quentin.

Eleven

Shortly before seven o'clock the next night, the scene was set for seduction. Mouth-watering aromas wafted from Liz's kitchen to where she stood in the living room. The roast was in the oven, along with baked new potatoes lightly seasoned. Squash, fresh rolls and, her specialty, chocolate cake with mocha icing, rounded out the meal.

She held a match to the last candle, the one on the mantle. Candlelight always set the right romantic mood.

Blowing out the match, she turned to survey the scene. She'd moved her grandmother's antique table, just large enough for two, into the center of the room. An heirloom lace tablecloth graced the table, which was also set with heirloom china, crystal, and silverware.

Fortunately, her father had announced yesterday afternoon that he was going to pay an overnight visit to a friend of his in nearby New Hampshire and wouldn't be returning until tomorrow night.

He'd returned yesterday from his morning errands in an unexpectedly jovial mood, answering her questions with ''that's wonderful, sweet pea'' or ''whatever you like, Lizzie, honey.'' Her suspicions had been raised, of course, but she hadn't gotten anything out of him.

Well, if tonight went as she'd hoped, her father would have something to be happy about. Somehow that thought didn't bother her. So what if her father unexpectedly got what he wanted? She'd have Quentin.

She passed over to the mirror above the side table to check her appearance one last time. She'd bought the black lace negligee and matching filmy robe with Quentin's reaction in mind. If his past reactions to her lingerie were anything to judge by, she was right on target with the armor she'd chosen for battle.

She stared critically at the face that looked back at her. Her hair curled past her shoulders and framed a face currently dominated by wide, anxious green eyes. At least her lips still appeared perfectly lined in a shade of wine.

All in all not bad, she decided, but she'd better cut the anxious look. If Allison had done what she said she would, Quentin would be here any minute.

Right on time, the doorbell rang. Liz sent up a silent prayer as she walked to the door on unsteady legs.

Quentin looked dumbfounded for a second when

she opened the door. Then his gaze flicked over her, a hot intense look in eyes that seemed to heat wherever they landed. Finally, he extinguished the twin flames, and his mouth set into a hard, thin line.

"Allison wanted me to stop by on the way home from the office. Said you had some books for her." His eyes narrowed. "But I see this is a bad time."

Bad time?

One second she was flustered and feeling the flush to the roots of her hair, the next she was confused. Then it dawned on her that he didn't realize she was waiting for...him!

Quentin continued to glower at her belligerently, yet words of explanation wouldn't come and she found herself moving aside and saying simply, "Come in. I'll get the books for you."

Once she closed the door, the little entryway seemed dominated by his presence. She was also mortified to discover that the cool evening air had caused her nipples to pucker and jut through the thin silk she was wearing. She felt his gaze like a brand.

"Lead the way," he said, his voice sounding a little strained.

She turned and went toward the living room, her mind racing, all the while aware of his deliberate tread directly behind her. Why did she feel like he was ready to pounce?

When he spotted the cozy little table illuminated by candlelight, he said coolly, "You're expecting someone."

"Er—yes. Yes, I am." Her voice sounded breathless to her own ears.

"Not Lazarus." He made the words nearly a challenge.

She almost laughed. That the thought would even enter his head gave a little boost to her confidence. He showed all signs of being jealous. "No, not him."

"Not that it's any of my business," he said, seemingly biting out the words with effort, "but is it anyone I know?"

"Yes, you know him. Quite well in fact."

A muscle worked in his jaw. "Can't be Matt or Noah. They know I'd kill them," he muttered, almost musing out loud.

Really, she'd have to thank Allison later. Whatever Allison had said, it was clear she'd led Quentin to believe he wasn't the man Liz was expecting to ring her doorbell. In the process, Allison had given her a much needed boost of confidence. "I can't believe you'd do bodily harm to either of them."

"You're evading the question."

"Who do you think it is, Quentin?" she said softly, her heart flipping over.

Their eyes met and she knew the love she felt was shining through her eyes.

"I know who I want it to be, dammit." In two strides, he reached her, enveloping her in his arms as his mouth descended.

She kissed him back, putting her soul into it, even as the tears slipped from beneath her lashes.

"God, sweetheart, don't." He cupped her face and caught the tears with his lips. "Don't cry. I'm not worth it."

His tenderness just made the tears flow faster. He

kissed her cheeks, her eyes, and made forays back to her mouth in between. "Elizabeth."

"You g-gave me the s-stock," she sobbed.

He cupped her face. "That's why you're crying?" He gave her a lopsided smile. "Honey, I'll give you whatever you want. Name your terms."

He looked so sweet and endearing, she blurted, "I want you. I want you to love me. To love our baby."

He stood stock-still as if she'd hit him over the head.

"I love you," she whispered.

He grinned suddenly and then leaned his forehead against hers. "You've got me. All of me. Heart, stock and barrel." He drew back and wiggled his eyebrows suggestively.

Her laugh came out as a hiccup. "That's an awful pun."

He gave her a soft kiss. "I love you."

Now it was her turn to look shocked. "You— No, that's not possible."

He chuckled. "Why not?"

"You said you were done with that romantic love stuff, that it was much better to treat the whole thing like a business proposition."

He tucked a loose strand of hair behind her ear. "So I did. I was an idiot. You broadsided me, sweetheart. I had it all figured out, and you came along and scrambled the whole puzzle again. By the time I'd sorted it all out, the pieces were in different places and the picture looked a lot different."

He looked suddenly sheepish. "And maybe I was

just feeding you a line that sounded good because I was desperate.''

"Desperate?'' she echoed.

"Yeah, desperate to stop you from going ahead with the whole sperm bank idea while I had time to figure out why it kept mattering more and more to me what you did.''

His words sent a thrill through her, but she couldn't help asking, "What about Vanessa?''

"What about her?'' His brows drew together. "She bruised my ego, and, yeah, I got very cynical about women for a while. But I realized that what I felt for her wasn't nearly as strong as the feelings I had for you.''

"You so much as talked with that idiot Lazarus—'' Liz tried hard to hide a smile "—and I got jealous. Not to mention hitting the roof when I found you having dinner with Noah—'' He broke off at her smile and shook his head ruefully.

"You really thought Noah and I…''

"Yeah, I was really far gone.'' He sobered then and said, "I should have told you about Donovan Construction—''

She placed a finger on his lips to silence him. "I don't want the stock. I realized after your lawyer called that the company wasn't nearly as important to me as you are.''

He nodded. "I didn't want you to think you couldn't marry me because I owned the damned company.''

"Yes,'' she said softly, "I know and that meant the

world to me. You also made me realize that I had nothing to prove.''

His eyes glittered and then he smiled. ''I'm glad you recognize that. You're an entrepreneur, Elizabeth. Don't ever doubt it.''

''I cried when your attorney told me about the stock.''

He frowned and shook his head. ''I didn't think the reaction would be tears. I guess I'll never understand women.''

He really was a sweetheart! Not to mention being devastatingly attractive and the father of her unborn child. How lucky could one woman get? ''Don't worry. I intend to spend a lifetime giving you lessons.''

She was rewarded with a quick grin. ''Oh, yeah?'' he said, his voice dropping an octave. ''I think I'm ready for the first one.'' He swept her up in his arms and she had no choice but to link her arms around his neck as he headed for the stairs to the bedroom upstairs.

''The roast—'' she protested.

''—can wait.''

A wave of heat swept through her. He was carrying her up the stairs and she made one last attempt to explain. ''I cried when your lawyer called because your giving the company stock to me made me hope that you cared and not just about the baby. Then I realized I loved you so much, the company didn't matter. What I wanted was you. That's when I decided to seduce you tonight.''

''Thank God for that!'' He looked down at her appreciatively as they entered her bedroom. "I promise to be willing and eager prey," he add huskily.

He took off his suit jacket and tie and then came down on top of her on the bed, nuzzling her neck, his hand stroking up her thigh.

"Who's supposed to be seducing whom?" she asked breathlessly.

"Ah, Elizabeth. I can't keep my hands off you."

She laughed helplessly. "That's what got us into this situation to begin with, if I recall. The fact that we both couldn't keep our hands off each other."

He moved her filmy robe aside so he could kiss a shoulder. "Mmm." His lips trailed up the side of her neck and she turned her head to give him better access. "Let's take it slow and make it last this time."

His lips moved to her mouth and gave her little nibbling kisses. When his hand moved up to cup her breast intimately, her eyes fluttered shut as she let herself delight in the feel of his hand kneading her soft flesh. "Ah—" she swallowed a gasp as his thumb traced over her nipple "—I'm a little more sensitive now."

He lifted his head, and his eyes, already smoky gray with arousal, met hers. "Yes, I can tell." He paused. "Could you take my mouth on you?"

The question and the image it evoked was so erotic, she shivered and her already distended nipples jutted even more prominently beneath her negligee, as if asking for him to do what he had only voiced till now.

"Oh, please, yes."

He smiled, seemingly pleased at her enthusiasm, and slowly moved his hand over her shoulder and down her forearm, taking the thin negligee strap with him and exposing her breast to his hot gaze. "You're getting more assertive. I just hope that I can keep up with you—both in bed and out."

"Or die trying," she teased, echoing his words when he proposed that they enter into a business arrangement to get her pregnant.

"Or die trying," he murmured, his eyes never leaving hers as his head descended and his lips closed over one nipple. His tongue swirled around the peak and then began a steady sucking motion that had her hips rising off the bed as delicious sensations rippled through her.

His hand moved up her thigh to inch the bottom of her negligee farther up. She felt his erection pressing against her and moaned softly. When he lifted his mouth from her, she lowered the strap of the negligee that had remained in place so his lips could find her other breast.

His hand sought the spot between her thighs and she moved her legs apart to afford him access, sighing when he cupped her and began moving his palm in slow circular motions against her warmth.

She pulled his shirt from the waistband of his trousers and moved her hands beneath it to caress his back. His hand against her moist heat was fanning the flames inside her.

It was time, she decided, to give as good as she got.

And with that thought, she moved her leg against the bulge in his trousers, stroking him through the fabric until he lifted his mouth from her and groaned.

"You know, for someone with only a couple of sexual experiences, you really know how to pack a punch!"

She looked down at herself and then at him. "You're wearing too many clothes," she teased.

"That's easily remedied." Standing up next to the bed, he undid the buttons of his shirt and took it off, then raised his arms and lifted his undershirt over his head, tossing it on the floor to meet his shirt.

When he started on his belt, she stopped him. "Let me." She wanted to undress him, to peel away the layers, as she'd spent years longing to do.

He let her undo the belt and lower the zipper of his suit pants before he stepped out of the trousers, kicking off his shoes and socks in the process. When he pulled her up against him and gave her a soul-searing kiss, she twined her arms around his neck and gave herself up to it, glorying in a dream come true.

When they finally came up for air, he groaned, "God, sweetheart, I've got to have you."

The words sent tingles along her nerve endings. They both had the power to affect each other deeply, but, she realized, she trusted him in a bone-deep, instinctive way.

Lifting her negligee over her head, she tossed it on the floor to meet his shirt. "I love you, Quentin," she said throatily. She skimmed her fingers over his chest and down his forearms, emboldened by the power he had infused her with. "And I'm going to show you how much."

Her hand rubbed against his erection, stroking him through his boxer shorts, before she divested him of his last piece of clothing and caressed him with her bare hand.

His eyes closed and his breath hissed between his teeth. "I don't know how much more 'showing' I can take...." he warned.

She laughed softly. Would she ever have imagined even a few months ago that she'd literally have Quentin in the palm of her hand?

His eyes opened. "What's so funny?" he said roughly.

When she shared with him what she'd been thinking, he pretended annoyance. "Oh, yeah?"

"I was just teas—oh!" Her sentence ended in a gasp as he tumbled her to the bed.

His hands made short work of the black silk panties she wore, and then he was trailing kisses down her body, between her breasts, and lower.

When he rose over her again, he muttered, "I can't wait, Elizabeth."

"Then don't," she whispered and drew him down to her, her legs opening so that his erection was hard against her. "Make love to me, Quentin."

"Lord, yes."

Quentin probed against her until he found her opening. Slowly he eased himself inside her, gritting his teeth against the urge to go faster. She was so tight and warm, he was having trouble not losing his mind.

Elizabeth's legs came around him and took him in the rest of the way, until he was buried in her warm wetness. "Oh, Quentin!"

Her sigh of pleasure was nearly his undoing, but he

forced himself to go slowly, sliding in and out of her steadily and deliberately.

She was everything he ever wanted, everything he ever needed, and he groaned with the effort to hold off his climax.

Liz rubbed her hands over the sheen of sweat that glistened on Quentin's skin. She breathed in his musky male scent, kissed his shoulder, and rubbed her breasts against his chest. He was making her almost mindless with need.

His eyes were shut, his jaw clenched, his breathing labored. She gripped his hips, sinking her fingers into his flanks, and urged him to go faster, her hips rising to meet his thrusts. The tension coiling within her was almost unbearable.

"Elizabeth, sweetheart, let me—"

Before he could finish, she found her release, unwinding against him and crying out.

Quentin felt his mind shutting down. Instinct took over as he drove himself into her until the world exploded. He collapsed against her, spent but replete.

"I love you," she whispered.

"Let's never stop saying it, sweetheart."

Epilogue

"**H**ow the mighty have fallen." Noah Whittaker shook his head at the sight of Quentin pacing back and forth in the living room of his house, three-week-old Nicholas Patrick Whittaker snuggled on his shoulder, emitting periodic burps as if on cue from his father's gentle pats on the back.

Quentin troubled him with one quirked eyebrow and a sardonic smile. "You don't know what you're missing."

Noah grinned and nodded when the baby burped. "Right. Fortunately, I don't."

Quentin was getting used to his brother's teasing. These days nothing could puncture his sense of blissful contentment. Opening his heart to Elizabeth had been the best thing he'd ever done. And the birth of Nicholas had just cemented that happiness.

"Fortunately you don't what?" Allison asked as she entered the room followed by Elizabeth.

Noah lounged back on the sofa and pasted a beatific look on his face. "Er—fortunately I don't have a thing to do besides watch Quentin burp my fantastic brand-new nephew."

Allison looked skeptical, causing Quentin to hide a grin. He turned as Elizabeth reached for the baby, and they exchanged loving looks. Motherhood had left her glowing from within—helped along by a healthy dose of love from him, he liked to think. He gave her a quick kiss as he handed the baby over.

"Ugh," Noah grunted in good-natured disgust. "The resident love bunnies at it again. Don't you guys ever give it a rest? You'll be giving Junior here a brother or sister before he's crawl—"

Allison interrupted, "Watch it, pal. You never know when you'll be next."

Noah pretended to look offended. "You'd wish that—" he jerked a thumb at the picture of connubial bliss created by his brother, sister-in-law, and nephew "—on me?"

"I have the most *da-arling* friend," Allison said sweetly. "You'll love her, really you will."

Noah raked fingers through his hair. "I should have never become an accomplice to your plotting," he grumbled. "I should have known once you knocked off ol' Quent here, it would be just a matter of time before you got around to me."

Liz turned to her friend. "Well, I guess I do have to thank you for originally suggesting Quentin as a sperm donor, as crazy as the idea sounded at the time."

Noah guffawed. "That was the tip of the iceberg."

Liz saw Allison's guilty look even as the suspicions started to creep in from the edges of her mind. "What does Noah mean, Ally? Tip of the iceberg?"

Noah smirked from his position on the sofa, and started counting off on his fingers. "Well, let's see. First, there was the plot to lure Quentin to the French bistro and make it seem like you and I were on a date."

Allison glared at her brother, and Liz's jaw dropped open. "You planned that?" she asked Ally.

"Then there was the plan to throw you and Quentin together with weak excuses like having Quentin pick up cocktail party decorations for Allison from you," Noah went on with equanimity, obviously enjoying himself.

"Noah, you know you're going to pay for this, don't you?" Ally asked in a voice coated with artificial sugar.

Liz swung to her husband. "Did you know about all this?"

Quentin shrugged. "I suspected some of it." Then added dryly, "But I'm sure there are details of the master plan that I'll be finding out years from now."

"Yeah," Noah agreed, "and then there are details that not even Allison could have foreseen. I mean, who knew that Elizabeth's father and Celine would hit it off? Patrick's moving back to Carlyle and I doubt it's only to be closer to the baby. Those two will probably be heading off to the land of wedded bliss soon, and, Ally wasn't even trying to get *them* married!''

Allison finally threw up her hands. ''Okay, okay. I'm guilty as sin. I admit it.'' She shrugged. ''What are you going to do? Sue me?'' With a sly glance from Liz to her brother, she added, ''As far as I can tell there would be no damages awarded anyway.'' She glanced at little Nicholas dozing in Liz's arms. ''Unless you think my darling pint-sized nephew is a bad outcome?''

Liz looked down at her now sleeping son and her heart swelled. She and Quentin had created this miracle together, a product of their love for each other, which continued to grow every day. She glanced up as Quentin slid his arm around her and knew he could read her answer—identical to his own—in the love in her eyes.

''No, Allison, this isn't a bad outcome at all. Thanks for helping us along a little,'' she said before raising her face for her husband's kiss.

*   *   *   *   *

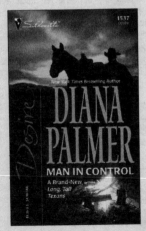

Silhouette Desire®

COMING NEXT MONTH

#1531 EXPECTING THE SHEIKH'S BABY—Kristi Gold
Dynasties: The Barones
The attraction between Sheikh Ashraf Ibn-Saalem and Karen Rawlins, the newest Barone, was white-hot. But Karen wanted control over her chaotic life—and a chance at motherhood. Ash offered to father her baby, but only as her husband. Dare Karen relinquish herself to Ash…body and soul?

#1532 FIVE BROTHERS AND A BABY—Peggy Moreland
The Tanners of Texas
Ace Tanner's deceased father had left behind a legacy of secrets— and a baby girl! Not daddy material, confirmed bachelor Ace hired Maggie Dean as a live-in nanny. But his seductive employee tempted him in ways he never expected. Could Ace be a family man after all?

#1533 A LITTLE DARE—Brenda Jackson
Shelly Brockman was the one who got away from Sheriff Dare Westmoreland. He was shocked to find her back in town and at his police station claiming the rebellious kid he had picked up—a kid he soon realized was his own….

#1534 SLEEPING WITH THE BOSS—Maureen Child
Rick Hawkins had been the bane of Eileen Ryan's existence. But now she was sharing close quarters with the handsome financial advisor as his fill-in secretary. She vowed to stay professional…but the sizzling chemistry between them had her *fantasies* working overtime.

#1535 IN BED WITH BEAUTY—Katherine Garbera
King of Hearts
Sexy restaurateur Sarah Malcolm found herself in a power struggle with Harris Davidson, the wealthy financier who threatened to take her business away. But their heated arguments gave way to heat of another kind…and soon she was sleeping with the enemy….

#1536 RULING PASSIONS—Laura Wright
Consumed by desire, Crown Prince Alex Thorne made love to the mysterious woman he had just rescued from the ocean. But when Sophia Dunhill ended up pregnant with his child he insisted she become his wife. Could his beautiful bride warm Alex's guarded heart as well as his bed?